The Magical Flower of Wishes

and other short stories

The children of
James Brindley Community Primary School

FOREWORD

Looking into the mind of a young writer is a privilege. Predicting the future of each young writer is fascinating. Those children who have chosen to put their thoughts down on paper, re draft, edit and finalise their work, have been brave and excited in the task that they undertook.

The third volume of stories from the children of James Brindley Primary School is once again, packed with promise for the reader and the writer in equal measure. Children who have written stories in our first two volumes have gone on to write more and publish their own work independently. I hope that the children who, for the first time, are published within these pages, feel proud enough of their achievement to be encouraged to repeat the process many times in the future.

We hope you enjoy these original works by the children of James Brindley Community Primary School.

Mr Moore
Headteacher
James Brindley Community Primary School

http://www.jamesbrindleyprimary.com/

CONTENTS

ACKNOWLEDGMENTS

Thank you to all the children that submitted stories for this book and to the families who encouraged and supported you. You are now published authors and this is *your* book.

THE MAGICAL FLOWER OF WISHES
BY KAMILLA FARIA-SOARES

It was a dark stormy night and the lightning crashed and banged, making everyone wake with fear. The rain hit the ground like thunder as the wind rustled in the air making whoosh noises. Suddenly, within the blink of an eye, something shiny like a diamond fell to the ground from the sky. Boom! And in that exact same place, the ground started to rumble.

In no time at all a flower sprouted from the ground. Now, this flower was not an ordinary one; it was a magical flower that possessed the power to grant wishes. The flower was so beautiful and each petal was a different colour- red, yellow, pink, blue and purple. Five different colours on five petals. This magical flower knew that someday someone would find her, look after her, and make wishes.

When it was morning, the sun shone bright like a yellow crystal in the blue blanket-like sky. Sofie woke up with a huge smile, remembering that it was the weekend. Sofie was a typical eleven year old girl, her eyes a lovely shade of colour of chocolate brown. Her lips were a soft pink and her hair was cinnamon chocolate brown. To any onlooker, she was a regular girl wearing the regular clothes that an eleven year old girl would wear. As Sofie got off her bed, her mother rushed into the room.

"Thank goodness you're awake, Sofie, because we're going shopping."
"But Mum," Sofie cried, "isn't it early to go shopping?"

Sofie's mum pointed at the clock; it was one o'clock. Sofie looked shocked and surprised at what she has saw.
"How come I slept that long?" she said and to Sofie's amazement, her mum had the answer. "Well, Missy. You were awake all night watching a movie with your dad. You went to sleep really late."

Sofie remembered that she has been awake all night watching a movie with her dad. With no fuss, Sofie went to the kitchen, poured some fresh milk from the farm, put some cereal in the bowl, sat herself down and began to eat. After that, Sofie went to her room to dress into her clothes then met her mother, who was already waiting for her at the door and was tapping her watch. In no time, Sofie was out of the house. Sofie and her mother always walked the twenty- five minute journey to the shops.

On the way, Sofie saw something shiny near a bush. It was the shiniest thing Sofie had ever seen. It was the most beautiful flower ever, adorned with five petals – one red, one yellow, one pink, one blue and one purple.
"How come no one noticed this most beautiful flower?" Sofie said with amazement "Well, it's mine now."
Sofie ran to her mother with the flower, "Mum, look; isn't this the most beautiful flower you have ever seen?"

Sofie's mother looked at the flower, "Wow what an interesting flower. Come on, Sofie; the shop is just down the road." Next to the shop there was Sofie's favourite bakery shop. They would always stop at the bakery before going shopping. After eating some yummy, sweet, delicious pastries or bakery they finally went shopping.

The shop was massive; it had everything you could need- like food, clothes, books, shoes, and furniture. Sofie wasn't interested at all, however; she was engrossed by the flower. "That's weird. I've never seen this flower in any of my plant books. After about one hour in the shop, they were about to go home when Sofie stopped her mother, asking if she could have a pretty vase for her flower. Her mother looked annoyed.
"Sofie, you already have a vase at home."
"But, Mum" Sofie begged "please can I have a

prettier one?"
"I said no."
"But."
"No buts."
"Please," she cried. And with that she turned her back on her mum.
"Alright," she moaned, "I will buy you one"
"Yes, you're the best! "she cried.

Sofie's mum bought her the vase she wanted. Finally, they finished shopping and, when they arrived home, Sofie couldn't wait. She rushed to her room with the vase and the flower. Sofie was about to put her flower in the vase when her mobile phone rang- it was Tiffany, her best friend from school. Sofie forgot that she was holding her vase. As she reached for her mobile phone from her pocket, the vase crashed on the floor. There were just broken pieces scattered on the ground. Sofie cancelled her call with Tiffany. She stared at the broken pieces then sat next to it and began to cry. "I'm so foolish. I should've been careful. Now Mum's money was wasted. That was my favourite vase. I wish I could mend the vase somehow. I wish I could." With that, the flower started to glow. It glowed so bright that it could blind you. Surprisingly, some wind came and mended the vase in the blink of an eye. The red petal fell. Four petals remained. Sofie looked in awe at what had just happened. She had the power to have anything in the world. She was the luckiest girl in the world and was filled with happiness.

Sofie decided that she must take a walk to decide what to wish for. She told her mum and set off. As she was heading to the shop, an idea popped in her head. "I wish that I had the best clothes." Nothing happened. But then money appeared in her pocket. Sofie screamed with delight. Everyone watched her dancing and hugging her money. Some thought she was crazy.

Sofie decided to go shopping. When her best friend came, Sofie wasn't paying attention. "How are you doing?" Sofie was too busy thinking of what to buy. "Sofie, I'm raising money for charity. You have to see the poor children suffering in far off places. "I'm sorry to be rude but I don't have extra money. I only have the money that I want to spend on clothes so I can't help you. And about those children… they can live being poor because they are already poor. I can't live being poor because I'm not poor. I can't live being poor, if you see what I mean.

"But, Sofie; they can't live being poor. You should see how they suffer. Children's lives are more important than money. The African children are starving. You have to see Africa for yourself to see how they suffer."

Sophie replied, "Maybe I will visit Africa to see but I just care about money. I don't need you either because I have my money and you're just annoying." Tiffany was in tears. "You're a monster. I don't know what money did to you, Sofie. I don't know." And with that, Tiffany ran away. Sofie's heart did not agree with what she had said. Inside the shop, she thought that she should visit Africa so she got out her flower. "I wish I was in a country in Africa."

A strong wind came and carried her away. It carried her to a poor country in Africa, dumping her head first on the ground. Sofie got the flower but unfortunately a strong wind came and carried the flower away. "Noooooooooooooo!" Sofie shouted. "I want to go back home. How am I going to survive this place? This is like punishment. Maybe it's because I was selfish.

Sofie walked, trying to see if she could see a village or a market, but realised she was lost. Sofie walked for what seemed like an hour before she couldn't take it any longer. She sat down on the sand clutching her stomach, crying with hunger. Sofie had never been so hungry before. "Oh, I'm so hungry," she cried, "this is the feeling of being poor." Surprisingly, there were orange trees nearby. Sofie couldn't wait. She dashed to them and managed to get some fruit by pushing the tree until they fell. Greedily, Sofie tossed some oranges in her mouth. "Yum, so tasty. I want some more." Sofie pushed the tree again, releasing more oranges.

While gobbling up her delicious, scrumptious oranges, she spotted a tall, ugly man carrying children with their arms tied up. The furious man put the children - who were in tears - in a sack then got out some equipment for capturing children. A child Sofie had just spotted was playing near the orange tree with his friend. She saw how skinny they both were compared to her. She knew that it wasn't their fault because it was almost impossible to find food here. But the man approached them and, with a swoop, kidnapped both the poor children. Sofie heard the children shouting in the sack, yelling and crying at the same time. "He must be a kidnapper!" Sofie exclaimed. I must save the boy and the other children". Sofie stopped eating. She went and followed the man, who kidnapped yet another child. She was desperately searching for a plan when an idea popped into her head. *What if I get some oranges, knock him over and let the children escape? Then, while I'm running, collect some more to throw at him to slow him down to give us more time to escape.*

Sofie went and collected enough oranges then went close behind him. SPLAT! Sofie threw oranges at him. The man's eyes were stung with the acidic orange juice. "RUN!" Sofie yelled as she continued to throw more oranges at the man. The children understood. They ran and Sofie ran too, picking fruit on the way. "Ngiyabonga," they called (which is 'Thank you' in Zulu language). The kidnapper gave chase. Sofie ran even faster, fearing for her life but the man seemed to catch up with her even though he was slipping on the pieces of fruit. The man spoke angrily in his own language. Sofie could tell that he was angry with her. The poor girl ran for her life. "Aaaaaahhhhhh!" In front of her was a policeman. Luckily, Sofie dodged him by skidding under his feet. The kidnapper, meanwhile, collided with the policeman. If the policeman hadn't been there, Sofie couldn't have escaped.

Sofie ran to a clearing, away from the kidnaper and policeman. A wind came. It was blowing a flower to Sofie's hand- the flower of wishes. Sofie held the flower like it was a precious gift from heaven. She began to shout now, "I wish I was back home." The strong wind blew Sofie back. Before she returned home, Sophie went to her friend's house to apologise. Tiffany answered the door,

"Oh my gosh. It's you. Everyone was worried about you. Where on earth, have you been, Sofie?"

"It's a very long story indeed," Sofie mumbled.

Tiffany made her best friend comfortable and even asked if she wanted tea. When she'd finished making it, Tiffany gave a cup of tea to Sofie, "Your mother was worried sick. She called the police and the police were searching for you."

Tiffany paused, sipping more of her tea, before she continued.

"Everyone was searching for you and when your mother heard there'd been no sign of you she fainted."

"My mother fainted? She *actually* fainted? Oh dear!"

"You said it, alright. Then, when she woke from her faint, she still couldn't stop worrying."

"Tiffany, I don't get it. Why are you not mad at me for the mean things I said to you?" asked Sofie.

"I was, until your mother rang asking if you were with me. I knew something was wrong and that, deep down, you didn't mean what you'd said to me."

Sofie stood up. "I have to go home and show my mum I'm okay because she's obviously been very worried."

When she arrived home, Sofie burst into tears.

"Mum!"

"Sofie!"

As the mother and her daughter hugged, the mother burst into tears.

"Where have you been, Sofie? I was so worried."

"It's a long story."

"It doesn't matter as long you are back home, Sofie."

In that moment and in that day, Sofie learned a valuable lesson - that you can't get what you always want and that it's important not to want too much. From that day on, Sofie made sure she learned her lesson. Every time a wishing flower grew, she made sure her wishes were selfless.

AVA AND THE WEATHER WONDERS
BY IMOGEN WOODARD

One warm summer's day, as the mist was just clearing, a girl called Ava, who was in year 6, was walking downstairs to make her own breakfast, which was pancakes and syrup because her mum and dad had gone to work. As she looked out of the window, she saw a UFO that she thought looked as if it belonged to some gang of aliens! The faint sound of metal clashing together, as if someone was sword fighting, met her ears; she could hear blasters being shot as well. Thinking about all the things the aliens, with their blasters and swords, could do to her, she shoved her last bit of pancake into her mouth. "Silly me", she thought "I'm making this all up!"

Just then there was a knock at the door, rat-a-tat-tat. A wave of realisation crashed into Ava, and trembling with fear, she slowly began to walk to the door, and opened the door a smidge. Seeing that the alien UFO was turning to land right outside her house, hovering between her neighbour's garden and hers, she slammed the door shut. Ava began to panic, she wished her mum and dad were here. Rat-a-tat-tat! When she plucked up enough courage to reveal herself, she opened the door...

To her surprise there weren't aliens coming out of the door: there were humans! They looked like they were superheroes - they wore black cloaks and a red suit, and the superhero to the right had a dog at his heel. They each had a different symbol of weather on their chest. The symbols were lightning, rain, sun, hail, snow and ice. Ava had stood there speechless and amazed for about ten seconds before she started to talk unsteadily. "What are you here for?" she asked in a confused way. Then one of the heroes took over speaking as he could see that she was lost for words. "I am Bolt, the lightning symbol, this is Storm the rain symbol, this is Lumin the sun symbol, this is Hailey the hail symbol, this is Frosty the snow symbol and the dog is Polar, the ice symbol." Lumin started to speak; " We all have different powers. I'll tell you them later. Anyway, we need your help, we need you to join our team." Ava was amazed, she was thinking *Why would they pick me to be part of their team?* She was just an ordinary child. Lumin spoke, "Please come on to our team. A few weeks ago we lost one of our team members and placed missing posters all around the country to help us find them. Come on Ava, you're our only hope." Ava finally decided she was going to adventure far and wide and she didn't need any more persuading. She ran upstairs, packed her bag and was off! She couldn't wait until she was in their UFO. She had already made friends with Polar the dog; he was jumping up at her and bouncing on to her knees. She was finally on the UFO which was absolutely massive. She could see the signs on the doors that said Tantalising Training Room , Scintillating Sleeping Room , the Diminishing Dining Room, the Captain Control Room and the Rescue Gear Room.

Ding dong, said the loudspeaker "Evil Grabthorn goblin is on the loose in the village centre!" Ava was going on her first adventure with the Weather Wonders. They set off ready for the expedition to defeat Grabthorn. They went into the Rescue Gear Room and they all put on their invisible armour over their suits and then got into their jetpacks. Lumin and Ava helped Polar with his. Then they set off to the Captain Control Room and started up the engine. The group also steered their way into the village centre.

Ava had her first sight of Grabthorn. He had scaly skin and green prickly thorns all over him. The superheroes and Ava took swords and other equipment from the gear room for the battle. Grabthorn was trying to put thorns on all the plants that animals and humans ate so that they would have no food to eat. Ava and the superheroes jumped out of the UFO and shouted to Grabthorn to stop, but he refused. *Clang! Clash!* went the swords as they battled against Grabthorn. Grabthorn defended himself by shooting lasers which released thorns into their paths. Eventually though, Grabthorn was cornered and the Weather Wonders were finally able to tie him up and throw him in jail. Polar the Ice Dog released a blast of freezing air which caused all the thorns to drop off the plants. Storm and Lumin together were able to make all the plants grow again to their ordinary size. All of the Weather Wonders shouted, "Generations of Weather Wonders have now defeated a hundred and one monsters all together! To celebrate, we are going to build an alien playground and Ava, we want your help to decide what equipment should go into it!" Ava was delighted that they had chosen her. After a while, she had decided to construct slides, swings, zip wires, trampolines, foam pits, climbing frames, a petting zoo and a free ice cream parlour.

After she had told the others what she thought, they got their building machine to do all the work in space so that the aliens could play in the new park. When it was finished, they travelled up to space and watched the aliens playing in it. The aliens looked really happy and thankful that the Weather Wonders had made this playground for them. They were so pleased with the designs that they decided to call it the Ava Park. Ava couldn't wait for her next adventure with the Weather Wonders!

CAPTAIN UNDERPANTS
BY ALFIE WHEELDON

Once upon a time in an ordinary town lived two ordinary kids called Cameron and Alfie. They went to a school called James Brindley Boarding School. Their teachers were called Mrs Butler and Mr Graham and they taught class Year 5G. The Headteacher, Mr Banks, was very strict and always shouted at people. So the boys went into the Teleportation Treehouse and made a transformation ring that they zapped their Headteacher with. Unwittingly, they also transported themselves to an evil world and when they looked at their Headteacher, he was now a man with his beard shaved off and wearing underpants. Cameron and Alfie put their heads together to try to come up with a name for their hero. Alfie had an idea to call him Captain Underpants.

Exploring this new world, they started beating all the villains up. *BOOM! CRASH! BANG!* All the villains lay weak on the floor- Cameron, Alfie and Captain Underpants were victorious. Then, from nowhere, a big talking toilet appeared from the skies above them. Captain Underpants greeted him with a big punch in the face!!!! Then the talking toilet arose from the ground, angrier and more powerful. A colossal battle began with Cameron and Alfie in the middle of it. They could see a switch inside the talking toilet's mouth and they somehow needed to get inside and shut him down.

Waiting for Captain Underpants to headlock the talking toilet, Cameron and Alfie struck. Alfie gave Cameron a boost to the talking toilet's knee before Cameron helped Alfie up. They clambered up to the mouth but there was nothing there anymore. Suddenly, they fell down his throat, into an evil lair. There was someone on a chair in front of them. Quietly, they went behind him, revealing that this person was controlling what the toilet did. The two boys had the same thought- *How about we subdue him and make the talking toilet shutdown?*

The chair spun round, revealing the evil genius at work. It was a person from their school. In fact, it was two. It was their friends- David and his evil assistant, Charlie. With a struggle, Alfie and Cameron subdued the evil geniuses. All that was left to do was shut the toilet down. Alfie used his computer technology and shut it down. Hooray! But then loads of tiny toilets scurried out. Captain Underpants used his laser eyes and shot at one of the toilets but it deflected the laser beam like a game of ping pong going from one toilet to the next. As that didn't work,

Captain Underpants used his earthquake stomp- he stomped on the floor sending an earthquake and wiped everything out. Alfie said, *How about we go back to our world?* So, the boys got their transformation ring and zapped Captain Underpants. And before they knew it, they were back in their school with their Headteacher still being very strict. In fact, nothing had changed. Alfie and Cameron were back at their school still getting up to mischief.

CAT OUT OF THE BAG
BY CHARLOTTE NANGLE

One day there was a girl called Ruby who had three sisters and two brothers. They were Liam, Luke, Renee, Rebecca and Rachel. They lived with their mum, Lyndsey and their cat, Calum. On Friday, Calum went for a stroll. He went to the Town Hall and met a girl cat called Amelia.

"Hi, what's your name?" enquired Calum.
The black cat with a white sock replied, "Meow, my name is Amelia."
"Who is your owner?" asked Calum.
"My owners are Emily and Carter," responded Amelia. Calum meowed and pawed goodbye.

By the time he reached home, he could smell his food. After finishing it, Amelia was waiting outside the door. Calum drank some milk and dashed outside where he spoke with Amelia for a short while.

"Well, I must be going. I can hear Emily shouting me. Goodbye!" and she kissed him on the nose as she left.

The next day, Calum dashed to Amelia's house and found three beautiful kittens. Their names were Liam, Ivy and Lee. In unison, they said their first Meow upon seeing Calum. Amelia and Calum were so proud. Emily and Carter dashed downstairs, hearing the meow.

Lyndsey and her children got in the car and looked for Calum. She went through the Town Hall and into a little neighbourhood where she found Calum at 14 Hyde Road. Lyndsey ran out of the car and grabbed Calum. She hugged him as hard she could. Emily ran out and wondered who had Calum in their hands.

"Are you this cat's owner?" Emily asked politely.
"Yes, I am." Amelia meowed.
"Is this your cat?" Emily quizzed.
"Yes, this is Amelia" came the response.
"There are some kittens down in the basement.
Would you like to come and see?"
"I'm sorry, I can't. I've got all the kids in the car,"
Emily replied.
"Bring them in!" came the response.

Lyndsey got Liam, Renee, Ruby, Luke, Rebecca and Rachel out of the car. They saw Liam, Ivy and Lee all asleep next to each other before it was time to leave. Calum went with her and said his goodbyes to Amelia, who kissed him on the nose.

ELEMENTAL DRAGON BROTHERS
BY CARTER GRAHAM & SAM SNEDDON

Hi, my name is Jack. I'm here to tell you about a legend that is believed to be about brothers. Oh, I forgot to mention that this story is based in Nagasaki, the largest city on the island of Kyushu in Japan. Okay, buckle your seat belts...

Far away, a mysterious weretiger approached a misty cave blocked by a huge boulder. The cave was located on the top of Dragon Peak, the peak where the dragons, Tornadeous, Guardian, Flameslinger and Kiushu sleep. As the weretiger, known as Gargantulus, opened the cave, it was now empty. "What, what... how?" He saw the past and then boomed, "No! Those pesky kids!"

Meanwhile, in North Korea, Amelia and Lee travelled through the thick snow. "That was a bumpy ride," said Amelia. The missing dragons had landed on a rickety old cottage, "This will do nicely" exclaimed

Lee. As they started cleaning the small house up, the door burst open and through the smoke a robotic voice boomed through the house, "We will destroy you!" Turning around, they saw robotic beavers carrying ice baseball bats. "Attack!" they all shouted as they charged. They were no match for Lee, however, who quickly reprogrammed the beavers. In a matter of seconds, the beavers started singing "We are robot beavers, we will take control" they said over and over again. "Okay, that's enough, this is just getting weird" said Guardian, bemused by the events before his eyes. "Hey, where has Kiushu gone?" questioned Tornadeous, "He was right here a moment ago!" Lee noticed that Flameslinger had also gone.

Back in Nagasaki, the cave of Dragon Peak had now been made into a secret lair, " Master" boomed a low voice in the dark, " I'm back" said Kiushu.
 "Ahhh, good; I have been expecting you" said Gargantulus as the dragons crouched in the corner. "Destroy Guardian, Tornadeous and those pesky kids" said the weretiger, now in human form. He had grey eyes, dark brown hair, four arms and a young looking dull face.

Back in North Korea, the dragons and the kids looked everywhere for the missing friends. "Hey, what is that in the distance? It looks like some sort of egg" said Amelia.
As Guardian flew up in the air he said, "It is an egg!" "What kind of egg?" shouted Lee, "is it a liquid nitrogen egg- an ice egg? Go and get it!" Guardian flew over and scooped up the egg... "It's hatching"

yelled Guardian, "Put it down then" said Tornadeous... Amelia immediately opened the egg, "Oh no, it's dead."

"Soon *you* will be dead, Guardian" boomed two very low voices. A ball of darkness hit Guardian. "Oh no, he's dead" said Tornadeous, "now I am mad" he said. Tornadeous then shot seventy balls of water at Flameslinger. "How do you like it, now your son is dead" said Tornadeoous in rage. "I will be back," said Kiushu as he flew away.

The team checked Guardian thoroughly. "He is definitely dead," said Lee, "I can't fix him".

The legend ends there. But it is said that Kiushu will return one day, when Tornadeous is older and wiser. That day may still be to come.

Regards,

Jack!

FRIENDSHIP ISLAND
BY SOPHIA ROIDITIS

This is a story about friendship and a wise Greek message in a bottle. The story begins on a lovely autumn day on the Greek island of Naxos.

Emma and her mother were on a girls' sailing trip out in the magical Mediterranean Sea but little did they know what adventure was lying ahead of them. Emma pulled out the picnic basket from under her seat and reached for her ham and cheese sandwich as her tummy was starting to rumble. Just then, her mother told her that there was a horrendous storm unexpectedly coming their way. They were very nervous.

Without warning the storm was over-head. Emma grabbed her mother's hand and closed her eyes tightly, hoping that the storm would go away as soon as possible. But it didn't. She opened her eyes hours later and they had been washed a-shore a tiny Greek island. Their boat was no-where in sight. Emma looked up and noticed a hand-made Greek flag above her. Someone else had been here...

All around, tropical palm trees were swaying lightly in the breeze. They were amazed by the scene in front of them. It was not like the other Greek islands, it was different, very different and it seemed like Emma and her mother were the only people on the island. They felt quite calm because this incredible island somehow made their emotions feel very different.

Emma and her mother explored the island for many hours and collected lots of tropical fruits such as figs and pomegranates as well as delicate shells. Suddenly, Emma glanced in front of them and spotted a transparent, glass bottle with something inside.
It was a message...

Emma felt shocked but excited at the same time. Her hands were shaking as she unscrewed the bottle lid and shared the massage with her mother. She read slowly,

Hello, I hope this message reaches Friendship Island. If it does and you are an unexpected visitor to our Island, let me introduce my friend and I. My name is Sophia and together with my friend, Angela, we created this Island. We understand that it may be difficult for you to leave the Island, so to help you we want to let you know that there is a secret door leading to a boat stored securely. Read on to discover where to find the hidden door:

The door is hidden
On this Island
The colours blue and white
Are key to your success
It is up to you now.
Follow this Wise Message*
We wish you good luck.

Emma and her mother stared silently at each other. However, before-long they had explored the Island, looking for the secret door. They were starting to feel tired when at last they discovered what they had been looking for, by the blue and white Greek flag! Emma pushed on the squeaky, old door camouflaged by the tree and it opened into a huge wooden garage where they witnessed an incredibly shiny, brand new speed boat. Emma remarked to her mother, "So this is how we get off Friendship Island. It's been great fun, but now I'm ready to go back home!"

Before they left, Emma wrote a thank-you note to Sophia and Angela, pushed it safely into the bottle and secured the lid tightly. She placed it carefully by the flag, hoping that one day the girls would return to their island. Thanks to the 'Wise Message' in the bottle, Emma and her mother returned safely to the Island of Naxos. The question was should they keep their adventure a secret or tell their family all about it? "No-one will ever believe what just happened to us," laughed Emma.

Author's Note:

True Fact – Meaning of Greek Names:

Sophia = Wise &

Angela = Messenger

Sophia + Angela = **Wise Message.**

HAVE YOU EVER WONDERED?
BY MARISSA CALDWELL

Have you ever wondered what's inside that old derelict depressing looking house on the way to your prison-like school? Well, if so, this is the perfect story for you. My friend Summer and I were on the dreaded walk to school on a cold and misty Monday morning whilst having our usual crazy talk. Suddenly, we heard a creepy crying noise to our right which spooked us both. The noise seemed to come from this old run down house. We always used to joke about this house being haunted but was it actually true? Instead of walking on like most children would, we stopped to discuss what we thought the noise was.

Due to our curiosity, and the fact that we were early for school, we decided to investigate. We approached the house- up to its old rusty gates, which stood out from the rest. Suddenly, we heard the noise again which sounded like a cry for help, possibly from an elderly person. Foolishly we decided to trudge up the cobbled driveway surrounded by overgrown weeds.

Summer then bellowed at me to look up at the window. Staring down at us from a gap in the closed curtains was what looked like a slim black figure with large green emerald eyes. I immediately became petrified of the creature before me and wanted to run away as fast as my legs could carry me but Summer persuaded me to stay. We again heard what we thought was a cry for help. We decided to knock at the door to see if everything was alright. We tried several times but no one answered. Then I decided to shout through the letterbox, "HELLO." Numerous times I did this but still got no reply. The calls for help became more frequent. We felt like we had to do something now as someone was in trouble. I tried the door handle and to our amazement it was unlocked.

The door was hanging on one battered hinge like a pendulum and it creaked loudly as it opened. There was an instant smell of damp which reminded me of the gear store at Lledr Hall. We made our way into the house; every room was dark and gloomy with cobwebs in every corner which caught specks of dust instead of flies. Every floorboard seemed to creek, making my heart pound faster, every second of every minute. We were so nervous and scared. The crimson red carpet was fading away and the gold and silver tassels were becoming lose, plummeting down the stairs like a waterfall. I started to edge closer to the stairs. The cry was becoming more constant and louder. We trudged up the stairs holding hands, making sure nothing happened. This was it, room 13. The sound was just on the other side of this large piece of wood. My hand gripped the handle and I started to twist it cautiously. Slowly I pushed open the large heavy door. Suddenly the curtains began to shake. My thoughts were racing. What was I going to do? BOO! A cat appeared with large emerald eyes and aggressively hissed at us, baring its fangs. We both screamed and ran as fast as we would in a cross country race down the stairs and out of the house door. We managed to get to school just in time for the whistle.

So, if you have ever wondered what's inside an old derelict depressing looking house- now you know. Just make sure you don't go in!

LAND OF THE DEAD
BY ELIZABETH EDEN

"Please, Mum", I pleaded for the tenth time today. "Well, okay, but you and your friends must be very careful". So I called my friends, Kamile, Grace, Lauren, Isabelle and Blake. I said "Hi, do you want to camp in the forest together?" They said yes. So I quickly packed my stuff and met them all later that day. Of course we all had tea with our family first, but after that we went to the forest.

We all sat near the warm and cosy fire as we told our scary stories. After that, we went to sleep but on the stroke of midnight, I heard some beautiful singing and when I opened my eyes I saw shining, colourful, glowing lights in the moonlight. Astonishment raced through my blood. There they were, the fairies. I quickly woke up all my friends and we watched them for 4-5 minutes and then Grace whispered that we should probably go to bed now, so we did.

When we woke up the next morning, we looked at each other and realised we all had fairy wings. Blake had green, Isabelle had purple, Lauren had white,

Grace had pink, Kamile had red and I had electric blue. Blake shouted, "Why do we have wings?" Kamile whispered, "It must have been the fairies," in a deep voice. Suddenly, my phone rang and what a surprise- it was my Mum. I answered it and, as I was blabbering on with my Mum, we started to forget about our wings. When I was finished on the phone I said to my friends, "My Mum and your Mums said we can stay for a week". Blake gasped, "Thank goodness. I don't want to be seen in these wings!"

We all sat down in despair not knowing what to do next. After a while, I jumped up with excitement, "Think about it," I said, "we have all dreamt of having fairy wings before."

"I certainly haven't," grumbled Blake. "You must have dreamt of being able to fly though," I said. Blake thought for a minute, "Well yeah, I guess so," he finally admitted. "Well then, that settles it", I said, "We have a week before we have to be home and worry about people seeing, so until then why don't we just enjoy having wings?"

Kamile, Grace and Isabelle jumped up in a whirl of excitement. Blake took a bit more time to agree. "First things first" said Grace, "We need to learn how to fly." We all started looking around for a good spot to jump off. Kamile spotted a tree on the other side of the stream that would be perfect for climbing and jumping off. We didn't know how to cross the stream without getting too wet but Lauren saw some stepping stones. We all made our way to the stepping stones to get across the stream to the tree- we all got across nice and dry. Well, all of us apart from Blake; he was still moaning and not paying attention so slipped and got a bit wet. He wasn't hurt so we all laughed, even Blake.

When we got across to the tree we were all excited to climb up and jump off to fly. It didn't work though; we all fell to the floor with a crash. "It's no use!" groaned Blake.

"Wait. What did Peter Pan do when he learnt to fly?" asked Grace. "He cheated- he had Pixie dust!" said Blake. Grace looked for a minute before saying, "Yes, but we have wings. He had to think of a really happy thought, let's try that. But remember it has to be something that makes you really happy" Grace said happily.

A happy thought. For a few minutes they all stood thinking until one by one they came up with something that they thought would be a strong enough memory and happy enough to work. "I'll go first" Isabelle exclaimed. So she took a jump and she could fly! We all had a go and it went pretty cool.

Our happiness didn't last very long though. That evening we were all playing by the stream, showing off at how well we could fly, when a strange looking man came over to us. He had a long curly brown beard that went all the way down to the top of his yellow boots, his hair was long too and went down to his belt and he had a very peculiar outfit on. He had a hat that was nearly as tall as him and he had a strange outfit on that made him look like a Viking.

He walked towards us and stopped when he got close enough for us to hear him. "You must act quickly, you are in great danger," said the strange man. "My name is Theobald and I am here to warn you," he continued. "You have been given wings by an evil wizard called Doctor Death. You have those wings for a week and then if you stand in the stream a week from when you first got your wings, then they will disappear and you can go back to your normal lives. But for the magic to work you each have to be holding a magic time stone; your stone must be the same colour as your wings but the evil Wizard has hidden them in the Land of the Dead." We all looked at each other wondering what would happen if we didn't get the stones and after we asked, we got a horrible answer. "Well, if you don't get the stones before midnight, a week after you got your wings, then you will have your wings forever. But after the week you will belong to Doctor Death, your wings will turn black and become heavier each day and you won't be able to fly. Soon you will all be very sad," finished the man.

We had all been so happy until we found out that there is a darkness with people having wings- the King of the Darkness, the nightmare of all nightmares, Doctor Death. So we had to go on a mission to the world that you shall never speak of, the Land of the Dead. That morning we packed all the gear that we would need. We had heard that the Land of the Dead was a dark and cold place so we made sure we were well wrapped up, all had a torch and had enough food and drink.

We had to find those stones before it was too late. We followed the stream, the way Theobald had told us to, and like he said we came to a big strange looking tree that was twisted and grey. To get through to the Land of the Dead, we had to stand in a circle around the tree, hold hands and say three times, "Hakora, hakora take us to the Land of the Dead." After the third time, everything started spinning, until we finally all fell in a heap on a cold, damp floor. We jumped up and looked around; everything was dark, cold and made us feel sad. We set off to find the stones and we wanted to do it quickly to get out of this creepy place. Our wings didn't work here so we couldn't even fly.

We saw something shining not far away. We ran over and when we got closer we could see it was the red stone. "That was easy", said Blake. He climbed up the stairs to get it, but, as he got closer to it, the stairs turned into a slide and he came tumbling down. "Oh," said Blake, "it wasn't as easy I as thought." After a long time of us all trying to reach it, we tried doing it all together so when the steps turned into a slide we could push each other up. After the fifth time of trying it like that it worked and Grace grabbed the stone. "Great," shouted Grace happily. "Here, Kamile, this is yours" said Grace.

We looked around trying to see another stone. "There!" shouted Isabelle. She was right; we ran over to see the green stone lying at the top of a small fountain. It looked easy to get but we thought it would be a trick like the last one so walked up to it slowly. We were right. Every time we tried to grab the stone all the water from the fountain turned to ice and the stone was stuck in the middle. "Now what?" I asked. "I know," said Lauren. She went in her backpack and got out a flask with her hot chocolate in. We all looked at her, wondering what she was doing now. Lauren told us to get ready to grab the stone and when the water turned to ice she tipped her hot chocolate over it so it melted the ice and we could get the stone. "Yes!" shouted Isabelle and she gave the stone to Blake.

It took us longer to find the next stone, and this one wasn't as easy to get to. The white stone was balanced on the point of a very tall building. Lauren was excited to see her stone but we didn't know how we were going to reach it. It was even surrounded by sharks. One of us had to swim through the sharks and climb the building, so I said I'd do it because I didn't want my friends to get hurt. "Thank you so much" Lauren said in a relieved voice. Well, after that it took me an hour to get the white stone because I was too much of a wimp to try to get it at the start. When I did get it, we all cheered, especially Lauren.

A gorgeous lagoon took our attention so we wondered over to take a look. It was beautiful and there- right in the middle- was the purple stone. "Well, at least mine is only surrounded by mermaids" said Isabelle. Kamile looked for a minute and then said "They are not ordinary mermaids, they are pure evil". Our wings don't work here so we could not fly across to the small island in the middle where the stone was laying. We all thought, not knowing what to do until Kamile had an idea. "Okay, I have a plan!"

said Kamile enthusiastically. If you all go to the other side and distract the evil mermaids then I will quickly swim across at this side and get it without them seeing. We ran round to the other side and pretended to try to get in. All the evil mermaids surrounded us straight away. They were very nasty; Kamile was right. They were trying to pull us in to the lagoon to drown us. Thankfully, we didn't have to stay near them long because Kamile was really fast and got the stone in just a few minutes. "Thank you so much, Kamile" said Isabelle.

There were two stones left, mine and Grace's and we were losing energy the longer we were in the Land of the Dead.

We saw Grace's pink stone in a candy floss stall. It wasn't that easy to get though because it was surrounded by candy floss zombies. We had to use some magic Nerf guns to shoot them down so we could get to the stone. It was fun- a bit like a video game- but it was scary because it was real and the zombies were really fast. We didn't want to run out of bullets but soon found out that we couldn't because everytime we fired one, a new one magically appeared. We were all really good at aiming for the zombies but you had to fire hard enough and sometimes hit them more than once for the magic Nerf guns to work and turn them back into humans. We wasted a lot of time here. It took us nearly 3 hours and we were really tired when we had finally got all the zombies out of the way. Isabelle was closest to the candy floss stall in the middle, so she leant over to grab the bag with Grace's stone in it but, before she could, another zombie we hadn't seen jumped up from behind the stall and Isabelle fell backwards on to the floor. Blake quickly shot the last zombie twice and Isabelle managed to grab the bag. Grace was so happy now. There was only my stone left to find.

Suddenly we all felt icy cold and the wind started blowing harder. When we looked we saw a dark figure walking towards us. It was Doctor Death himself. He looked at us and laughed evilly. "None of you can leave my land until you have all six stones and you will never get the final stone" he said nastily. As he walked away laughing evilly we saw a flash of electric blue and there it was. My stone was hanging around his neck on a piece of rope. "We will never get that," I said. "Don't worry, we will find a way" said Lauren.

Trying to come up with a plan to get my stone was really hard and we spent an hour trying to think before we came up with a plan. "So, we will dress up as his helpers, paint our wings black and then we will trick him into trusting us to look after the stone," said Isabelle. We didn't know if it would work but it was the only idea we had so we all decided to at least try because getting that stone was our only way out of the Land of Death.

We all went into his palace. It was cold and creepy and we didn't like being there. We finally found a cupboard and some guards, so we basically attracted them and then stole their clothes and locked them in the cupboard. Then we got in disguise. After that we went to Doctor Death and he was taking the stone off, ready for bed. When he started falling asleep, Blake quietly crept up to his side and gently picked up the stone and crept back out of the room. Once we were out of his bedroom, we all ran as fast as we could out of his palace. To get back we had to find a tree that looked just like the grey twisted one we found to enter. It took us 2 hours to find the tree. When we did, we ran over and got in a circle around it holding hands. To get out we had to say "Hakora, hakora take us out of the Land of the Dead" three times. We were so happy to land in a pile back near our camp site.

Our week was done because time flies in The Land of the Dead. We all stood with our stones in the stream and in a flash of light we were back to normal. We went to my house for tea. When we got back to my house, my Mum asked about our week then we started to laugh a little. I said, "You don't want to know- it is a long story!" So we didn't tell a soul about what happened that week. But we will never forget.

LAST KIDS IN WORSLEY
BY SETH CARROLL

Hi, my name's Seth. I was just a normal boy until they came. Are you wondering who they are? I'll do a recap for you then.

I lived a normal life with a normal family, in a normal school called James Brindley. My best friends were Calum, Carter and Sam. We liked to think we were pretty special, but actually we were just normal boys, annoying (according to our parents) but normal.

Things were going pretty well, until one day as I walked out of school I heard a terrible groaning sound. I turned round to ask somebody what it could be, but instead you won't believe what I saw. It was only the freakiest, most terrifying thing you could ever imagine (and no it wasn't my Mum). It was a Zombie! It tried to grab me, but I dodged it and ran as fast as the speed of light to the treehouse in my back garden and climbed quickly up the ladder. I heard screaming everywhere. I sat there panicking, not knowing what to do for what seemed like forever. I must have eventually fallen asleep because I woke up the next morning and looked cautiously out of the little window. It was like a scene from one of those post-apocalypse action games. I crept out of the treehouse, deciding I needed to go and look for Calum as I couldn't face this alone. I set off for Calum's house, making sure that I didn't let my guard down for a second.

I made it to Calum's house in one piece. I'd normally knock but I didn't want to alert anything lurking inside. I carefully and slowly opened the door. It was deathly silent. I crept up the stairs. Finally I reached his room. The door was closed. I could hear the faint sound of breathing from inside. I swung open the door to catch whoever was inside by surprise. To my surprise, BONK!!!! I was hit on the head by a flying light sabre.

"Seth, what are you doing? You scared me to death!!!!" shouted a terrified Calum.
"Sorry," I said, while rubbing the bump that had rapidly appeared on my head. "I had to know you were alive."
"Well I'm glad you're here because I have something to show you," said Calum.

I followed him downstairs and out into his back garden. There was a massive car with weapons and armour all over it.

"Where did you get this from?" I asked.

"Don't worry, they're not real guns," he answered.

I excitedly jumped into the driver's seat and revved

the engine.

"You don't know how to drive Seth!" Calum said frantically.

"My Dad can do it so it can't be that hard. It feels like we are in Transformers, we should call it something," I said, thinking of a name.

"That is already done my friend," said Calum boastfully. "Meet the Dark Destroyer!"

We decided we should take the Dark Destroyer to the shops and get supplies for weapons. On the way there, we made a few tincy, wincy bumps. Okay, by that I actually mean we crashed into wheelie bins, broken fences, fallen trees, etc.

When we were about half way there we saw something in front of us. At first we thought it was another zombie,but when we got closer we discovered it had white skin. We got out to see what it was. It was Carter!

"Carter!" I shouted.

He looked our way and came running towards us. When he finally got to us I asked him how he had survived.
"I lived off the food in my Mum and Dad's van," Carter answered.

"Well, we were just on the way to get some supplies for the treehouse if you want to come with us?" Calum said from the car.

"Is Calum here too?" Carter asked.

"Yes, so are you coming with us?" I said eagerly.

"Sure, why not?" he answered.

When we got to the shops, we went straight to the Co-op (which is where my Mum used to work). We got some Sumas, apples, Twirls and M&Ms. Next, we went to B&Q to get some stuff to make amour and weapons.

We were on our way out of the shops when we heard something that sounded like growling. We all agreed that we should go and investigate, so we all crept round the corner and looked through the windows of the cinema where the noise was coming from. We sneaked inside and upstairs to where the screens were. As we went slowly past Screen One we heard the growling again but louder.

As we entered the cinema, there, lying in front of the screen was a humungous green monster. It wasn't growling, it was snoring! We tiptoed over to examine it. While we were doing it, Carter accidentally stood on an old piece of popcorn. One of the creatures bulging eyes opened and looked straight at us menacingly. It got up on all fours.

"Run!" Calum shouted and we all burst through the doors and out of the cinema.

For a moment we thought we'd lost it but then the monster came bursting out of the cinema walls.

"Blarg!" it screamed and started chasing after us.

I remembered that we had bought a nail gun in B&Q. As I was about to pull it out of my backpack, the monster spat out acid. A bit of it caught my foot and I fell to the floor in pain. Quickly, I rummaged through my bag and found the nail gun. I pulled it out and aimed it at the monster's legs. Without hesitating, I pulled the trigger. The nails flew through the air and hit the monster in the leg. It collapsed on the floor in agony, but then quickly jumped up and threw itself at us. This time I shot it in the chest and it staggered back onto the edge of the banister and SPLAT onto the floor below. We looked over the banister to see if it was still alive, but it wasn't moving. We all breathed a sigh of relief and ran out.

While we were on the way to the treehouse, Carter said, "When the monsters and zombies came, I saw Sam run back into school."

"When we get to the treehouse do you want to reload and go and look for him?" I asked them.

"Yes," Calum and Carter said at the same time.

So we went and got armed up.

At the entrance of the school we heard something inside. We barged inside and there (wait for it) was a zombie ball!!!! We ran as fast as we could up the stairs and into Year 5 and locked the door. We saw Sam crying in the corner.

"Hi Sam," I said.

"I'm not leaving here!" he said.

"Why?" Calum asked.

"Because my parents saw me run into school," he explained.

"Okay, we'll just leave you to starve, shall we?" I said.

"Okay, okay, I'll come," he said casually, even though I know he was desperate.

We somehow managed to avoid the zombie ball and get to the treehouse safely in the Dark Destroyer.

We will all have to get used to surviving and dealing with monsters.I have a feeling it will be harder than we think.

LILY AND THE MAGIC BALL
BY IMOGEN PATTISON

Once upon a time there was a little girl called Lily. She always played by herself as she didn't have any friends and she always got bullied. All she really wanted was to have at least one friend who was kind to her.

One day she found a ball in her garden. She picked it up, wondering where it came from. The ball felt warm in her hand and suddenly she found herself in a field. It was dark, damp and creepy so, a little scared, she started walking until she saw a wolf. It sat still, staring at Lily. Its coat was grey and white and it had green eyes. Lily's heart started to quicken with fear at the wolf. She didn't know what she should do. The ball was getting hotter so she decided to be brave and tossed the ball over to the wolf. Then, to her surprise, the wolf started digging into the ground. He pushed the ball into the hole. Lily didn't want to lose the ball so she ran over and knelt down to try to get the ball out, when suddenly the ball began to glow and it became hot; it created a light path leading through the dark field. The wolf looked at Lily, started to follow the path, then stopped and turned to look at Lily again. Lily wondered what to do. Should she follow the wolf? The wolf's eyes appeared human-like, so maybe the wolf would help her find her way.She really didn't want to stay in this dark, creepy place, so she got up and walked behind the wolf.

After a while, feeling less scared, she noticed the field started to become lighter and brighter with lots of flowers and butterflies. *This place is so pretty*, thought Lily, as they came to a cottage with a beautiful garden. She followed the wolf through the gate, along the garden path. The wolf beckoned her to go inside and then followed her in. The inside of the cottage was just like Lily's home; in fact, it *was* her home. She turned around and saw the wolf transformed suddenly into a white ball of light and there appeared a girl like herself. 'I'm Sophia' she said. She smiled at Lily and said, "Welcome home, friend, I've just moved into the house next door."

MY CONFIDENCE
BY RUBY STEVENSON

Hi, I am Sarah and I had a bit of trouble yesterday. In fact, a lot of trouble. As well as being troublesome, it was confusing and weird. You're probably wondering, *Sarah, why are you just using dumb words such as confusing and weird? You should just tell us the story from start to finish.* Well, you're in luck because, I am going to tell you the whole confusing story.

It all started when my twin sister Sienna said that I was dumb and weird. Suddenly I thought, *Why in the world would she say that?* Was she jealous of me? I never knew until I asked her. Unfortunately she cried, *Why would I tell you?* Then a thought pinched my head and, the thought said maybe she was jealous after all. That thought made me over the moon (not exactly). I could not believe that I was right all along. So, I decided, to go to, the Trafford Centre to give myself a makeover.

Once I got there, I went to the most popular shop (I think anyway) - TOP SHOP. In the corner of my eye there were these kind of jeans- HIGH WAISTED JEANS. I thought I needed to get them because, I noticed that all of the popular girls, wear those kind of jeans and they look outstanding on them. But suddenly, these mean girls caught my eye. They were gazing and laughing over at me. People saw on the outside of me that I was strong and tough but in reality I am isolated and weak and think I've no future in my life. I stormed out of the store thinking that I am a shameful and a loser. I kept on calling my mum to try and pick me up but she could not understand me because I was drooling all over the phone whilst crying. My mum told me to breathe and then speak my words but instead what happened was like when you breathe on a glass window and steam comes up. That was me but with a phone.

A COUPLE OF HOURS LATER . . .

I was all calmed down but I was still feeling hurt inside. But then, I heard a knock at the door. It was Sienna. She passed me an oddly shaped present which. I rapidly tore the wrapping paper to reveal what was underneath. My eyes turned to be like an owl's eyes when I saw the gift. It was the high waisted jeans that I was looking at before I saw the mean girls. I tried them on. Once I tried them on I suddenly felt extremely more confident and that will never ever change.

54

I WILL SEE YOU NEXT TIME BUT UNTIL THEN, BYE FOR NOW!

NINJA SCHOOL
BY SOPHIE POTTS

It was a normal day at James Brindley but something extraordinary was about to happen. Some children were keeping a big secret; they were actually the children of secret ninjas. Blake, the flash of us all, is the son of Mrs Farrow; Kristian, the comedian who is the son of Mrs Read; Imogen, the story teller who is the daughter of Mrs Booth; Carter, the Spiderman who is the son of Mr Graham; and last but not least, Sophie, the Hulk of us all, who is the daughter of Mrs Potts. Together they are the JNL. The Junior Ninja League. They were at the school because they had to stop the evil Mr Stanfield. But he has a plan and noone knew what it was.

The mission had begun when Mrs Potts the leader had found out that Mr Stanfield was a spy trying to escape the school. Mr Stanfield is actually the deadly Mr Octopus. The JNL were asked to spy on Mr Stanfield.

When all the children went to break, Carter and Sophie snuck into Mr Stanfield's room and saw exactly what they had expected. A cup of coffee. But it was not coffee inside the mug, it was a wooden dagger. Attached to the dagger was a map and on the other side, a plan. On the plan was a whole load of jumbled up words and a bunch of shapes. Although there was something Sophie could read and it was not good news for them. Miss Wilding was to lure the children in and hypnotise them. Carter and Sophie raced back towards the rest of the group. Along the way, Mr Moore caught them running and gave both Carter and Sophie a detention for running in the corridor. Once they got back, Carter spread the news to Kristian and Blake whilst Imogen was trying to gather their ninja parents. "Keep up the good work everyone." congratulated Mrs Potts.

It was hometime for school but not for the ninjas. Blake stayed behind to do some research. Sophie was also there, keeping a close eye on Miss Wilding. Sophie suspected that she was the leader of all the staff in the school and had turned them evil. Meanwhile, Blake had found the perfect book in the spooky library. *The history of teachers at this school* was the book's name. Blake and Sophie met up in their classroom and flicked through the pages. "Mrs E. Ward, Mr Moore, Mrs Jackson" muttered Blake, flicking through the pages. "Ahaa! Miss Wilding."

exclaimed Sophie. They were there all night long reading and had made a factfile.

The next day, everyone went to school early to get a head start on the day. Blake had brought his translator and translated the plan. "On the 1st of October in the afternoon is the day we will escape."

We all checked our phones …. "Today was the 1st of October." Everyone panicked. They all darted to Mr Stanfield's room. The children were already hypnotised. "He's onto us!" shouted Carter. They all rushed to tell the other classes but Mr Stanfield caught them. "Ger' off!" screamed Kristian. Sophie used her Hulk strength and tore Mr Stanfield away from Kristian. Then they darted away. But lurking round the blue painted corridor was Miss Wilding. Luckily, Blake had night vision goggles on and demanded Carter shoot her down with his webs. Miss Wilding tried to escape the dreaded net but she just got tangled even more.

In the melee, Mr Stanfield had escaped the school but that does not mean that the JNL can't catch him…

POPPYFIELD BLITZ
BY NIAMH KERRY

A gang! It just consisted of Aria, Eliza and Amber not including the boys- Jack, Max and Scott. I'm also in the Stupid Seven. Sorry, I forgot to introduce myself; I'm Elisabeth, Lizzie for short. I hate when people call me my Christian name. Being eleven, I love misbehaving. What's wrong with creating some mischief? Naughty is my middle name! I bolted down the terrace-my dark, brunette hair swaying behind - the subway was only down the street. My handbag was crammed with spray paints of all colours .Crimsons, violets, oranges, indigos, roses and emeralds - and a two pound coin. We were only decorating it - weren't we? Thrusting out a scarlet can, I pressed on the nozzle, writing (In chalk duster style) Blitz! Little did I know … It was so much fun. We were sniggering. Laughing. Joking. Just having fun.

Nobody could see us as it was a subway. We were under a major A-road. Jerking, Aria tossed another can to Scott; he then chucked it towards me. Trying to avoid it, I smashed into the 'redecorated' wall and rapidly sunk to the cold, concrete flooring. I lost consciousness almost instantly. My head was whirling around. I clutched my coin. Blitz. Blitz. Blitz. Blitz.

Stirring, my eyes opened. *Where am I? Where is the subway? How did I get here?* Numerous questions drowned my other thoughts . This is not Manchester. Or Liverpool. Or Leeds. Or London. A boy parted the innumerable amounts of rubble and sprinted right through. "Hey You," I screamed. He just carried on running. How ignorant! My senses slowly taking hold again, I noted his vintage clothing. How odd! Typical weird folk. All my clothes were from big name brands. They certainly were not moth eaten and threadbare. Dressing up day I suppose. I glanced downwards. *OMG!* A torn chestnut brown dress hung off my shoulders, and it had white lace around the collar- what an absurd combination! What was that? A cardboard satchel kinda-thing hung off my right shoulder. Curiously, I peeked inwards! It was like a mask. Black leather and goggles and a bizarre dotted circular thing. Pieces of a strange jigsaw were slowly piecing together. A group of grimy kids ducked down behind some debris. "Where am I?" I requested. "London, East End" came the rigid reply. "What year?" I questioned. "1941," came the puzzled reply. *1941. The East End.* This was way too much. There were bombs and fire and raids. How could this have happened? I turned over my hand hoping to find my two pound - it was now a guinea.

A horrific sound pierced my ears- it was louder than an ear-splitting fire alarm. All the people in sight were rushing towards the tube station! *Why a station? Think back Lizzie, think back.* Great grandma Florence always had talked about the Underground being used as shelters. Hurrying towards the station, I noticed a mountain of beige sandbags. As I ambled inwards an abundance of bunks blocked the congested shelter. Babies bawled whilst some screamed and others shrieked. The mature wardens were hurrying everybody inside. Those with dogs were left with the dreadful decision, tie the dog up outside and be safe or stay with them and risk the bombs. How unlucky. They were left outside. I had never seen such a varying collection. Yorkshire terriers, Bulldogs, Fox hounds, Beagles and other ones I hadn't seen before.

Hours of tedious boredom. Most children were asleep. All the adults who weren't weeping were singing trying to keep our spirits up; they were having a positive effect on most but a negative on me. I couldn't help but thinking about the dogs. Ambulances roared in the distance. The wardens told me it was a heavy raid. Imagine if they were killed! I went across to the lavatory for some tissue to wipe my eyes. I took a step into the cubicle. Newspaper! They were using newspaper! They were short of paper! Ugh! YUCK!

Sleeping in the shelter was diabolical. At midnight I screamed. My first night in a cramped station. Someone told me to shut up too- they said the Luftwaffe was more active at night.

I woke in the morning to find destruction. A warden, who was wearing a gas mask, told us where our accommodation would be if our homes should be destroyed. After this, he told us about the bombed addresses- Berry Road, Laburnum Avenue, Dock Street and Poppy Drive (numbers 24-62). 753 people were killed in the attack yesterday with 1216 injured. One woman howled in anger. Another collapsed in shock. I was sympathetic to those who had died in the raid, but happy for those who had escaped. I couldn't be evacuated as I was new to the area and, besides, I really needed to help the dogs. There were broken wedding photos on the ground and fires that blazed onwards, turning the mahogany wood into smoking embers that swallowed every flammable thing in its presence. I sauntered towards the docks. *How could people cause such destruction?* How horrible. Hours after, a quarter of the dogs were still there after the raid. *What could I do? Could I leave them? Who would feed them?* I unknotted each of their leads then held them in one hand. *Where could I leave them?* There was a large school that had been abandoned a year ago after being badly damaged. Why not start up a rescue! *What should I call it? Could someone help?*

Day after day after day, I collected more dogs. Most were adopted but it was a never ending cycle of despair and hope. Only one was overlooked each time- Poppy- an Irish setter. I suppose it was because of her age (the others were mostly juvenile). There was a vast expanse of garden so it was no problem building the Anderson. I wanted to go back now! A colossal petrifying bomb fell to the ground. Everyone was in the Anderson but me. It swallowed me up like fire and let me go. Home!

Stirring, my eyes opened. *Where was I ? Where had the East End gone? How did I get here?* This was not the war. This was - familiar. I found myself back in the subway, bleeding but joyful. The only negative was Poppy- *Where would she be? Who would feed her? Who would play with her? What would happen if she died? Was it a dream ? No one would hurry her to the shelter?*

I was transported home in my mum's Peugeot and due to my phenomenal bravery she decided to take me to a dog rescue at long last. I had been begging for that forever! A dream had come true-well nearly There were no reputable ones nearby so I was allowed to look online. Battersea, Dogs Trust, RSPCA, Poppyfield! In the East End! On Poppy Drive! Was this the one I set up? It was still running! How? This was surprising! I looked further into the site - opened by Lizzie Chesterfield 1941. Wow! Would Molly still be there? "Mama, look- I opened it. Please can I go back?" I shouted from the back seat of the car. "How did you do that?" she said, doubting that I was telling the truth. You couldn't blame her, I suppose. I searched thoroughly for a perfect match. Hang on a second. Poppy. An Irish Red Setter. Surely not?

PUPPY OR BUNNY EARS?
BY GRACE CARROLL

Ruby had always wanted a dog. She had begged and begged her Mum and Dad for one but with no luck. So she was totally over the moon when her friend asked her to look after her Pug puppy, Fudge, for the weekend.

The weekend felt like it would never come to Ruby. Finally it was time to go and pick up Fudge from Hannah's house. Ruby had planned lots of fun things to do with Fudge and first on the list was a trip to the park.

Once they got home, Ruby ran around the house getting everything ready for Fudge's first outing. In her rush, Ruby nearly forgot the most important thing of all- money for the ice-cream van.
"Mum, can I have some money please?" Ruby asked extra nicely.

"Fine, but I've only got a £5 note so don't even think about spending it all!" warned her Mum as she reached in her bag for her purse.

Ruby walked out of the door looking very pleased, Fudge's lead in one hand and the £5 tightly gripped in the other.

At the park, Ruby let a super excited Fudge off the lead. As the puppy bounced up and down on the spot, Ruby realised that she'd forgotten his favourite ball. Remembering that Grandad always threw a stick for his dog, Ruby set off towards the nearest trees, followed by an impatient Fudge. Ruby found the perfect stick and was happily playing Fetch with Fudge until she heard the familiar sound of the ice-cream van. Eager to be first in line, Ruby ran off quickly, pulling her £5 out of her pocket.

"Please can I have a Bunny Ears?" Ruby asked as her mouth started watering. Ruby had waited a long time to order this type of ice-cream, covered in sherbet, with raspberry sauce dripping down, and not one, but two flakes stuck in to make them look like bunny ears. Without a second thought, she decided she should run back home and show her amazing ice-cream to her little brother. He would be so jealous.

When she arrived home, to Ruby's surprise, nobody seemed to care about the ice-cream. Instead they were looking behind her with puzzled looks on their faces.

"Where's Fudge?' her Mum shrieked, as a look of horror appeared on Ruby's face.

"He, he was be behind me," Ruby stuttered as she began to cry.

Everyone grabbed their coats immediately and ran out the door. Ruby dropped her ice-cream on the driveway in pursuit.

They quickly arrived at the park and frantically started to call Fudge's name at the top of their voices. When they had finally calmed down, they came together and made a plan to split up. Ruby went with Dad, and George went with Mum.

Dad and Ruby went to search everywhere they could think of. The bushes, the café, the lake, the play area, even under the skate board ramp, but with no sign of Fudge. When there was nowhere left to search, Dad and Ruby started to ask people if they had seen Fudge. Everyone had seen plenty of dogs but nobody seemed to have seen Fudge.

Mum and George had also had no luck. As they appeared from searching amongst the trees, George looked pretty fed up.

"I want to go home now Mummy," he said miserably.

"That's it, I know where he is!" Mum cried as she rushed off towards the entrance to the park. Ruby, Dad and George all followed her, trying to keep up but feeling very confused.

"Where are you going? This is the way to Hannah's house," yelled Ruby.

"Exactly!" shouted her Mum as she turned the corner into Hannah's road.

To everyone's surprise, there, sitting outside the gate of Hannah's house, was a very proud looking Fudge. Everyone was so relieved; they all rushed over and made a big fuss of him. They were just happy to have him back safe and well.

"I think we'd better put your lead on young man," said Dad, "we don't want to lose you again."

Together, they all set off for home.

As they passed the entrance to the park, Ruby again heard the familiar sound of the ice-cream van in the distance. Turning to her Mum hopefully, she said, "Mum, please can I have ..."

"Absolutely no chance young lady!"

REVENGE
BY ERIKA FOWLES

1 October 1968

It was about four weeks into Year 6 and it was not good news. Mr Grey was teaching Erika and Marissa again and they thought that he had got his memory back. Their collective suspicions had been aroused as he had been acting very oddly, watching them closely and following their every move from a careful distance.

3 October 1968

As Erika ran into school, the first thing she did was run to Marissa. They both squealed excitedly. It was tomorrow! Tomorrow was the day- Marissa's birthday. Erika was making Marissa a birthday card; she had also got her a present, but, every time anyone asked she said *Shhhh* and ran away. The day flew by as quickly as a bolt of lightning and it was soon time to go home. Mr Grey was being a bit strange; he was talking about letters, and a permission slip for a visit to Worsley Woods, whilst staring at them all.

4 October 1968

Yes! It was today. Running into school full of joy, Marissa stumbled into Mr Grey. He said that he had made her a cake. She was not sure about eating that. In the playground, Erika ran up to Marissa and squealed. She wished her a Happy Birthday and gave her a present- a brand new Barbie Doll. Marissa was about to tell Erika about the cake when the whistle blew. They were doing tests. GREAT, just what Marissa needed on her birthday.

Then Mr Grey brought out the cake. Marissa was just about to cut it when…it exploded all over her. Mr Grey gave an evil chuckle *"Ha ha ha."* He explained why he had made the cake explode; it contained a toxic gas to make them run faster.

They tried to get out of the classroom, but Mr Grey got Mr Russell (the Caretaker) to lock the door. Then Erika turned her eyes to the fire door. She suddenly made a run for it. She grabbed the handle and yanked the door open. The whole class ran to the door, charging out like a herd of elephants. They were in the fresh air now, but, had already inhaled the gas. Erika and Marissa could not remember the formula for the potion they'd made previously so they tried to guess.

5 October 1968

Erika and Marissa had been up all night trying to find the formula recipe. Suddenly Marissa yelled, *"I have it, I have found it- yeah."* They gave the antidote to anybody who had been affected by the gas. Once again life at James Brindley returned to normal (or did it?)

THE ADVENTURE
BY DARRAGH O'REILLY

Once there was a little boy called Darragh and he was on an adventure with his friends, Connor and Finn. They were on an adventure at sea, trying to find a shark, a great white shark.

Darragh had brought a fishing rod. He began fishing and hoped he would find a shark. After a while, they all decided to try the shark cage to see the sharks, but there were still no sign of any. Darragh spotted a lot of fish so he tried fishing again with Finn while Connor was taking a bath. Finn and Darragh caught a lot so they were treated to smoked fish for dinner.

The next morning they got up and had a look at their supplies and made breakfast. Darragh and Finn had toast while Connor had Cheerios. In the distance they spotted land, so they moored their boat and tried to hop off, but there was a massive wave that knocked them all out. They made it to the beach of a deserted island, but the swim to shore had exhausted them all and they passed out.

When they awoke, they saw bottles of fresh water, plates of fresh fruit and blankets. They were not alone... They shared the food and water and ran to the boat. Surprisingly, it wasn't broken, it was just damp. They all split up. Darragh went left, Finn went right and Connor went straight. They all met at a Temple. Darragh, Finn and Connor walked carefully into it. Stepping forward, Darragh made the first move while Finn and Connor stood still. It was pitch black. Connor and Finn heard Darragh's footsteps. And then they stopped. Finn and Connor walked towards Darragh.

Darragh tripped on a rock and lights flamed on, illuminating treasure that lay in the centre of the Temple. The boys ran to it but they heard, "Get off my treasure!!!" It was TUTANKHAMUN.

He chased them around the island, the boys running for their lives. Darragh and Finn undocked the boat and had begun to set sail when they noticed Connor wasn't on board. Finn stayed with the boat while Darragh dived into the water and swam towards the island. Watching from the boat, Finn saw Darragh run to the Temple where Connor was last seen.

After what felt like hours, Darragh emerged from the

Temple, Connor in toe. They jumped onto the boat and sailed off, away from the island.

When they reached the English Channel, Darragh said, "No wonder we could not catch any sharks! We are in the English channel!"

Finn and Connor huffed in anger. They turned the boat around and headed for the Pacific Ocean. Here they found lots of sharks including Great Whites. They went shark watching and caught lots of fish. They returned home and had a party, celebrating their survival and their adventure.

But who knows where Tutankhamun is...

THE END OF LOLA
BY LILY O'BRIEN

Excited, overjoyed and happy, Lola lay in her bed visualising what she would get with the treasure (gold) that she would find. Today, Lola was going into the forest to find treasure. Jumping out of bed, Lola put on her clothes, brushed her teeth and hair, put on her shoes, grabbed her stuff and off she went.

After an hour of walking, Lola finally approached the forest. As soon as she took her first step into the forest, she was literally screaming with excitement. She ran while following her map to where 'X' marked the spot.

Finally, she arrived at the spot when she heard something ruffling in the trees. Lola had no clue what to do. She tried to run back but she forgot the way and, to make matters worse, she had lost the map.
Lola started to move closer and the sound started to get louder. All of a sudden, something glowing popped out *What was it?* thought Lola.

It was a unicorn! Lola ran up to the unicorn and hugged it. She read the name on the collar in a confused voice. "Libby?" she said. "I like you, Libby," she explained. " In fact, I want to keep you. Come on, let's go now. Do you know the way out of here?" "Yes, I do know the way out. Come on, follow me," Libby said.

After 10 minutes of walking they were out of the forest. Lola showed Libby the way home. Once they arrived at home, Lola showed Libby to her mum- she was thrilled that she had came home with something.

So Lola went upstairs, got in her PJs, made a bed for Libby and off she went to sleep. In the middle of the night, Lola was fast asleep when there was a big crash downstairs. She made her way downstairs and found a black shadow. Before you could say 1,2,3, she was given a drink which gave the Evil Erika complete control over the unicorn's mind. Libby went upstairs, tied Lola up and took her to Evil Erika's lair.

When Lola woke up, she started screaming seeing that Evil Erika had captured her. But this time there was no way out. And that was the end of Lola's life.

THE FINGER MONSTER
BY HOLLY HUMPHRIES

CHAPTER 1

Once upon a time there lived a little girl called Holly and her Mum and Dad. When Holly was ten, her Mum and Dad told her when she went out never to go into the swamp. In the swamp there lived the Finger Monster. It was said that he loved eating little children's fingers. He would sit there eating fingers and, when he ran out of fingers, he would gallop off to houses in the night to try and steal some more.

CHAPTER 2

When the morning came, word spread that the Finger Monster had struck again. One day Holly and her friend Thalia decided to go into the swamp. When they reached the Finger Monster's home, Holly asked Thalia if they should look through the hole in the nest. Thalia said that she would look through. So she did and, as no-one was in the nest, she opened the door.

CHAPTER 3

Inside the nest they were surrounded by what looked like lots of fingers. Then they heard a noise. The Finger Monster was coming back. Holly saw a massive shelf and said "Let's hide behind there!" Just in time they ran to the shelf and hid but Holly knew that he had seen them. He went over to where they were hiding and bellowed "Who's in my nest?"

"We are", Holly and Thalia said. "We are just here to visit."

"Visiting!" he boomed.

"Yes" said Holly.

CHAPTER 4

"I've never had a visitor before", he said softly.

"Well, aren't you lonely down in your nest?" said Thalia.

"Yes, I am very lonely down here in my nest," said the Finger Monster, "everyone hates me."

"No, they don't," said Holly.

"Yes, they do. Everyone thinks I am evil. They say I eat fingers."

Holly and Thalia looked around the nest again and realised that the fingers were actually carrots!

"Well, we don't," said Holly and Thalia. "Why don't

you come out of your nest and come and meet people?"

CHAPTER 5

"Okay," he said softly.

So Holly and Thalia brought the Finger Monster out of the swamp and into the park. Holly, Thalia and the Finger Monster stood on the bench and Holly said "The Finger Monster is my FRIEND!" Everyone was shocked but then started to clap. Everyone loved him now and so did Holly's Mum and Dad!

THE FOOTBALL MATCH
BY ELLIS PINDORIA-STOTT

On the twentieth of March 2015, Manchester United faced Manchester City at Wembley Stadium. Forty five minutes later, the match started after a coin toss awarded Manchester City the kick off.

Ten minutes into the match, Aguero scored a beautiful goal in the bottom corner. On the thirty ninth minute, Wayne Rooney scored a sneaky goal down the middle; it was a beautiful sight. The half time whistle sounded loudly.

After the half time break, the match continued with Manchester United kicking off. Fourteen minutes later, United scored a wonderful free kick in the top bins; a spectacular strike. It was 2-1 with only five minutes left when Aguero scored a banger into the top bins, sending the game into extra time with a 2-2 scoreline.

In the first fifteen minutes of extra time, not one of the teams managed to score. It was the same in the second half of extra time so the game went to penalties.

Rooney took the first penalty kick scoring into the bottom corner. Both teams had five penalties and at the end it was 4-4, sending the game to sudden death. Manchester City went first and struck the crossbar. Up stepped Robin Van Persie for Manchester United, striking the ball right down the middle to score the winning goal; it was brilliant end to a brilliant game. In fact it was the best game I've ever seen.

But who went on to win the league? I'll save *that* story for another day.

GHOST TOWN
BY CAMERON HALL

On the Map of the World under the A of Atlantic Ocean is a little island called Camtopia. It sounds like a paradise- the sort of place where you would have your holiday. But, it is actually an island full of dirty things- a bit like a dump; wherever you go there is trash. The population is 13 but the 4 main people in this true story are Cameron, Alfie, Ellis and Ben (who is a chimney sweeper who never gets anything done).

The only mansion on the island is owned by Cameron, Ellis and Alfie and the smallest shed out of the mansion's 50 sheds is owned by Ben. The three men give Ben food, money and things to do his job right.

Anyway, the mystery began on March 18th when everyone went missing apart from Cameron- he was

81

left confused. He looked in Ben's shed. Nothing. The shop keeper down the street was also missing. Cameron needed desperately to find Ben. But when he searched for him, he found nothing.

Racing back to his mansion, Cameron frantically searched for his mobile phone. He found it under the mattress of his bed. He dialled 999 and expected to hear a calm voice on the other end. But no one answered. Worried, Cameron couldn't understand what had happened. Lost in his thoughts, he ran outside hoping to find someone, something – any living thing. Instead, he saw something in the distance. A pale light. He thought it was a figment of his imagination. It appeared slowly at first, before it took on human form. It was a ghost! The island was under attack!

Cameron woke with a start. Sweat poured from his brow. He breathed a sigh of relief. It had all been a dream.

THE HURRICANE
BY VANESSA SOARES

It was a dark and stormy night
The children shook with scare and fright
There was no sense of light - just lightning bright,
Sometimes struck right in to the ground.

The storm began to roar so loud
The wind blew stronger and stronger
Destroying all buildings and trees on its way
The people ran to safety in hope of escaping.

They left their homes, they left their cars,
They left their favourite places they loved to stay
The leaves of the trees blew all around
Making a wild and terrifying sound.

Some people cried, some people prayed,
Some lost their lives in the hurricane.

Some tried to fight, some tried to run
Some just decided to have some fun.
The next day after the hurricane,
People saw a massive flood
The humongous rain turned roads to rivers,
People were standing on their roofs
And waved for someone to rescue them.

The whole city was under the water.
People helped each other to get safety.
The hurricane left a very big damage to the city.

The sun shone – it was a hot, sunny day
The water dried out and
The river became the road again.

The people returned to their homes
They cleaned up the hurricane's mess.
They started new lives and they built new homes
With love and support.

THE MAGIC MAN
BY JASMINE WRIGHT

A long time ago there was a man. He wasn't an ordinary man; he was a very talented magic man. He could do all sorts of magic; he could make a rabbit disappear into a hat, or a frog jump from out of the sky onto his head at the click of his fingers.

But one day he went missing. His friends and family were distraught. Together, they put up leaflets about the incident, informing people of his disappearance. Despite this, however, he couldn't be found. Some people wondered if it could have been one of his magic tricks. Had a trick gone wrong? His family were desperately missing him and made signs to post around the community.

Shortly after, very far away, an old man was watching a magic performance on a park band stand when, out of the corner of his eye, he noticed a poster offering a reward of £1000 for information leading to the discovery of the missing man. Realising it was the performer he was watching, he approached him and showed him the poster. The kind old man took the magician back to where he belonged. His family were very relieved. But no-one ever found out how he had come to be in the park and where he had been.

THE MAGICAL ANT
BY RUBY PRITCHARD

Once upon a time there was a girl called Eliza. Eliza wanted every wish she made to come true. One day when she went to school, she wished she had a mint. So, when she went to bed, a magical ant came from under her bed and cast a spell so that, when she woke, a mint lay beside her on the pillow.

Eliza dreamed about different things every night. One evening she had a nightmare! It was about a sinister doctor called Mr Bloodflake- even his name was bad. Mr Bloodflake ate grass and mud. His cure for a cold was to eat tissue paper! Eliza dreamed that, as she was getting out of bed in the morning, she realised she had come down with a heavy cold. She went to visit Mr Bloodflake. He told her that to be cured she would have to put tissue paper up her nose. Eliza thought this dream was bad so she made herself wake up. She went down to breakfast and told Mum about the strangest dream she'd just been having. Her Mum told her to forget about the nightmare and they all lived happily ever after.

THE MAGICAL BOOK
BY ASHA MISTRY

She was five when she started loving books and she read them all the time. When it was her birthday, she got a book that was her great, great grandma's- it was very old. She started to read the book but there was something she didn't know about it. It had powers. Not just any powers, magical powers. The best part was that it could do anything she wished for. Incredible!

When she got to page 100 it had a picture of a wand but when she touched it, it came to life. The girl didn't know what to do with it, so she waved it around and around, then the wand started to vibrate. After a few seconds, she disappeared. The girl was spinning in something and it was like a tornado! She started screaming because she thought she would hit her head on the concrete floor. When she landed, however, it felt like she had fallen onto a huge pillow.

When she got up she realised she was somewhere she had always wanted to go. It was the cinema! She had always wanted to watch Beauty and the Beast on her own with the whole cinema to herself. Guess what, that happened. She had a huge tub of popcorn and lots and lots of sweets. Basically, she could get whatever she liked and go wherever she wanted.

The film started and she was so excited but, the only problem was, she wished that she could be in the film. However, she knew that was never going to happen. The next thing she knew, however, she was in it… in the film! She was one of the main villagers! All the characters looked fantastic, especially Belle who was beautiful. Even though she didn't have a speaking part, the girl was still happy because her wish had come true.

Suddenly, she thought about school and ran out, taking everything she had with her including the sweets. She ran straight towards the wand and it started to vibrate again. She went around and around and around. The girl wasn't scared because the last time it bought her to the cinema; she was now excited about her new adventure.

MONSTERS OF THE NIGHT
BY KATIE KEAN

Hi, my name is Katie and I am a spy. I have a best friend called Libby. There have been some really strange things happening at night and I am on an investigation to find out why. I try to forget about it but it just never goes away.

One night I was walking slowly down the street. It was dark and no-one was around. Suddenly, I saw a dark shadow quickly rush past me. I had a feeling I was being watched. Then my new phone went blank and started talking to me. It whispered "I can see you!"

The next day, I went to Libby's house. She is an expert on screens and science and is super-smart. So I asked her what could have happened. She told me that it must have been a monster. "It's strange that it never comes out in the day" I said. We decided to have a think about how we could stop it and then went to bed.

Unexpectedly there was a knock at the door in the middle of the night. Libby was asleep so I went and looked out of the window, but there was no-one there. The knocking went on all through the night and I didn't get a wink of sleep.

In the morning we went for a walk to the park. Libby spotted a beautiful butterfly so I took a picture of it with my phone, which was strangely fixed after the incident the night before. After that I took a few more photos then when we got home we had a quick look at them. Just then I had a brilliant idea. I could hide my phone in a lamppost then at night it would capture a photo of the monster…or the monsters!!! Then we could see what they were and what they looked like. "Come on, let's do it!" I cried.

The morning after we went to the lamppost to check the phone. When we got the camera there was a picture of the monsters. There were four of them. They were all small. They were all hairy. They all had four teeth and big eyes. One angry orange one. One silly pink one. One sensible blue one and one smart purple one. The only thing we needed to find out now was what they were afraid of so that we could scare them away. We decided to meet up in the park at night.

That night we met up and Libby was drinking a bottle of water. We walked around the park for five minutes and then sat down to talk. Suddenly we saw the Monsters of the Night! Libby screamed in fright and threw water on them. Three rolled away and one went

BOOM!!! "It exploded!" I shouted. "So that's what they were afraid of!!" yelled Libby, "Water!!"

The next night we met up in the park again. Libby had one glass of water and I had two. We swiftly threw the water on them. The first one went BANG! The second one went CRACK! And the third one went POP!!! We did it!!!!!

We went home and went to sleep. In the morning I thought, "That must have been a dream." OR WAS IT???

THE MYSTERY OF THE ANIMALS
BY JESSICA WEATHERSTONE

Once upon a time there was a zoo keeper. He was a kind man who cared for the animals and took great pride and care in his work. At night he would visit all the animals to say goodnight before going home to go to bed. In the morning he would come back to the zoo and visit each one in turn saying hello and feeding them.

One particular morning, however, to his great surprise, he couldn't find the animals. Not a single one of them. They weren't in their pens. They weren't anywhere. The animals had simply vanished. The zoo had to close. The local newspaper called it – the Mystery of the Animals!

Author's Note:
Would you like to be trapped all your life or would you prefer to be free? In the wide open world you can do what you want. Would you want to be a zoo animal that is endangered? Would you want to be last of your kind?

THE PUPMAID
BY YVIE COOPER

Once there was a pupmaid called Alaria and her mermaid owner was called Peppermint. Alaria and Peppermint lived in the sea with the other mermaids near Starfish Beach on Minia Island.

One bright sunny morning a sea witch called Zeteria set a tsunami on the mermaids' home! When the tsunami got to the mermaids they were all washed onto the sand, including Peppermint! So it was up to Alaria to save the mermaids, but of course she couldn't do it alone. Alaria called for her friends, two more pupmaids and three kitmaids.

"I need your help to save the mermaids" cried Alaria.

"But how?" said her friends.

"We need to go to Zeteria's lair and get the tsunami potion to make another wave to push everyone back into the sea" said Alaria.

"But we don't know what it looks like" said Fishee, the fluffiest kitmaid.

"How about we take all of her potions" said Wooll,

the smallest kitmaid, "we could use my wool ball to lasso all of them!"

"Great idea", said everyone.

So off went the six friends to get the potions and save the mermaids ... Zeteria lived in a cave at the bottom of Coral Beach on the other side of the island. The six friends used a sea-horse carriage to cross the bay.

When they got to Zeteria's lair, they sneaked under her potion table. Alaria could see that Zeteria was trying to make a flood potion! The other two kitmaids jumped out and distracted Zeteria by swimming around her head as fast as a sea-rocket, while Wooll lassoed every potion she saw. The pupmaids put the potions into sacks and they all swam back to Starfish Beach.

Zeteria fell in her cauldron because she was so dizzy after the kitmaids had left. "You will pay for this mess!" shouted Zeteria furiously as the six robbers swam away.

When they reached Starfish Beach, they checked the labels on the powerful potions so they could find the tsunami potion. They found it and poured the potion on the beach. This made a colossal wave which pushed all of the mermaids back into the sea.

All of the mermaids were saved!

THE STREET AT MIDNIGHT
BY REBECCA HARDWICK

It was a beautiful morning at Midnight Avenue where Rebecca lived. She was waving goodbye to her parents who were going on holiday to New York for the week. Suddenly the happiness in Rebecca was no longer there. She was filled with fright. Rebecca had to stay one whole week with her dreadful, creepy babysitter...

It was the night before the full moon and it was the first one that Rebecca's parents hadn't been there for and she was scared. She had a weird feeling every full moon that something would happen because of the road name. She had thought to herself many times that she was just being silly but then the doubts would set in once more.

Rebecca was sat at the table eating pizza in silence with her babysitter when it came to her; she had to think of a plan to see whether what she feared was real or not. Rebecca gobbled up her pizza, like a dog eating biscuits, so she could dart upstairs and into her room to plan how she could find out whether what she thought was true. To do this however, she would need some help.

In school the next day, Rebecca asked nearly everyone in her class to help her- apart from one group, the bullies. They had been bullying her ever since she brought up that she was scared. She went up to them (however, inside she knew she should turn back). She plucked up the courage and asked them but she wished she hadn't. One person, however, stayed still as the rest of the group walked away. It was Abbey; she said she would help Rebecca.

It was a cold, murky, tenebrous night at Midnight Avenue and it was the full moon. Rebecca and Abbey were in Rebecca's bedroom coming up with their plan of action. It was nearly time- there was only 2 hours to wait so they went outside to look at the street now. It was normal, like an ordinary day, but Rebecca knew in a couple of hours it would be totally different. Rebecca's babysitter was asleep on the sofa. Now all they had to do was sit and wait on the stairs, staring at the door. Abbey looked at her phone just as it turned to midnight. It was time. They took their last stride towards the door and opened it to find a normal street. They turned back to the house as Abbey heard something. Turning back to the street as fast as possible, the first thing they saw gave them a shock. A grave encrusted in moss rose from the ground and zombies were walking around the corner to the street. Did these zombies go around the whole block? Rebecca thought. Frozen, still in fright, they were urgently thinking of something to do. They turned to the door to run back into the house when they saw that Rebecca's babysitter had turned into a monster. They were screaming. What should they do? The zombies were closing in on them. To them it felt like they had been there for hours but it had only been half an hour when the zombies and graves went away and the zombie babysitter turned back into a normal babysitter. Needing to rapidly get away from Rebecca's babysitter, they darted upstairs. Silenced and in shock at what had just happened, they sat on Rebecca's bed.

Five days later, Rebecca and Abbey were best friends and Rebecca's parents were just pulling on to the drive. Rebecca was glad to see them and she desperately hoped they would not leave her on a full moon again.

TRICK OR TREAT
BY MATTHEW HUGHES

As I stared into the sky, I noticed the full moon. The air was orange around me. My friends and I were trick or treating in our town. We had heard stories of the old, rickety house that you should not go near. Ben dared me to approach the house and knock on the huge, black door. I wondered to myself - how bad would it be? It was only a dare...

Bravely, I crept towards the house (inside, however, I was petrified to go near it.) As I wandered up the path, the tree branches sprung out as if to grab me. Nearing the front door, my heart skipped a beat. I wished that I hadn't accepted his dare...

Raising my hand slowly and nervously, I reached out for the door. I could tell that my friends knew that I was terrified.
"No, come back!" cried Alicia, "It's not fun anymore, don't do it!" I was stumped. Should I go back or not?
"Don't be a scaredy cat!" bellowed Ben. Hesitantly, I

gently knocked on the door. Nobody answered. I knocked again. Suddenly, inside the house a light flickered. Footsteps approached the door. Bolts unlocked and the door creaked open. A tall, slender, old gentleman appeared in front of me.

"Trick or treat!" I shouted. I didn't mean to shout it but it just came out. When I turned around to look at my friends, Sammy had covered his face in fear with his hands. The gentleman stared at me. His bloodshot, hazel eyes focused just on me. My heart froze.

"Trick!" he exclaimed. From out of nowhere, a lady grabbed my friends and the man grabbed me. We were pulled into the house.

My friends and I were horrified. We had no clue why they had taken us. Alicia was trembling, Sammy was shaking and I knew Ben regretted his dare. They all looked at me in fear. I knew that I shouldn't have knocked.

"Hello there, children…" the man started, "You look… scared?"

"DON'T KILL US, PLEASE!" Ben screamed, "IT WAS ALL MY FAULT!"

"Don't be silly," the man replied, "I won't kill you!" His wife chuckled at Ben's sentence.

"We don't want to kill you…" the lady remarked, "We are just lonely!"

"So, you don't get many visitors?" I asked.

"No, we don't," the lady told me, "I made up that story as we dislike Halloween and didn't want to upset any children that knocked."

"Oh!" Sammy replied. We went on talking about what they did on Halloween. They told us that they turned all the lights off and stayed as quiet as possible. People ACTUALLY believed their creepy story.

RING RING Ben's phone was ringing. It was his mum. She told him that he needed to go home. After Ben set off, they told us why they were lonely. They said that their child had been knocked down on Halloween, which was why they hated it so much. He had been rushing across the road to another house. So intent on getting some candy, without looking, he stepped out in his dark costume into the path of an oncoming car. The panic-stricken driver could not stop his vehicle.

"How terrible," Alicia said, with a tear rolling down her face.
"Yes, that's heart-breaking…" I whispered.
She showed us an old newspaper article about the boy's tragic accident. The lady started crying. I could tell she hated Halloween because of what had happened. I really felt sorry for her. "That was him, his name was Greg…" she told us.
"My name is Dave," said the man, "This is my wife – Margaret."
"It was nice to meet you both, but I think we need to continue our trick or treating journey." I explained.
Margaret and Dave both waved goodbye as we left the house.
"Wait – I FORGOT SOMETHING!" Margaret shouted as she rushed outside with a bowl of candy, "Help yourself!"
We took some candy and waved goodbye. We

thanked them for everything as we walked away from their house.

"That story was sad…" muttered Alicia.

"I know…" Sammy replied.

"Yes it was..." I said, "But this Halloween is going to be the best yet!"

They nodded at me and we set off back into town. We went to lots of houses and had loads of fun.

"Well, only three hundred and sixty-five more days to go until we re-visit them!" Sammy shouted.

"Wouldn't they have forgotten us by then?" Alicia asked.

"Well maybe, so how about we visit them more often!" I said.

"Great idea!" Sammy remarked.

"Sure!" Alicia replied.

"See you guys at school tomorrow." Sammy shouted.

"See you!" Alicia shouted back.

"Bye guys," I shouted, "Bye…"

WHAT'S IN THE SUITCASE?
BY EMILY JOHNSON

It was Monday morning; it was the day Emily and her family had to return back home from their adventure of a lifetime in Florida. Emily reluctantly got out of bed and went for breakfast. Her dad asked her to shut the hotel room door on her way out but she got distracted by her little brother telling jokes and didn't shut it. Emily and her family enjoyed a nice breakfast. But meanwhile, something was going on. Somebody was creeping into their hotel bedroom!

When Emily returned to the room she barely had a minute to finish her packing. The family had a bus to catch to the airport and it was coming in five minutes. At the airport, Emily and her brother spent all of her last dollars in the shops at the airport buying plenty of presents for her family and friends. After a long tiring flight home the family were really tired and exhausted.

Emily grabbed her beloved Boro Bear and crawled into her cosy bed for a snooze.

After a long and peaceful snooze, Emily woke up. The familiar smell and feel of her own bed cheered her up. As she peered out from under the covers she saw two eyes peeking out from her suitcase. Just as Emily was about to scream, a friendly toothy grin emerged; she took only a second to discover that it was a young alligator.

Then Emily suddenly realised how her new friend had got there but she was still confused. How did it get past security? How strange, Emily thought. Walking slowly down the stairs, she held the alligator's hand. Downstairs, Emily got the lovely alligator some food and a bowl of water.

The next day Emily had school. During the night she'd had a dream that she took the alligator to school, so she did. In the morning she had literacy- it turns out alligators are actually quite good at literacy; they are like a walking dictionary. At lunch, the cheeky alligator ate all of Emily's friend's dinners and particularly enjoyed the fish fingers. After lunch, they had art and the alligator ate all of the pastels as well- this was not going well.

The situation was clearly getting out of control and unsure of what to do, Emily confessed everything to her Dad. Undaunted by the confession, her Dad called the local zoo and it was agreed that the alligator could live with a family of alligators that were already at the zoo.

The alligator settled in well with his new family and had lots of fun with his new friends. Emily would never forget the experience of living with an alligator and still goes to visit as often as she can, taking his favourite snack of fish fingers.

DESERT DOOM
BY CONNOR BUTLER

I was so excited when my mum bought tickets to go on holiday for a week. We were going to have a tour, on a plane, of Dubai. Also, I heard that they have cool sports cars and race cars over there. I love race cars. I might get a chance to go in one when we stop off. I've never noticed this, but my mum told me racecar is also racecar backwards!! Isn't that an interesting thought?

I got to the runway on a cold, frosty morning. The plane was magnificent. It had a really nice, old man who I found out was the captain of the plane and some complicated gadgets in the cockpit. My seat was so comfortable. The captain started the jet and we raced down the runway at a fantastic speed. Before I knew it, we were in the white, fluffy clouds souring through the sky.

As the weekend FLEW by, it was Sunday and time to land in the desert of Dubai. I was really tired and couldn't wake up. When I eventually did, I realised I was covered in dry sand. As I looked around I could see smoke everywhere. I saw the captain of the plane lying near me, a drip of wet blood trickling down his neck. All of the complicated gadgets in the cockpit had been blown up. Then out of the corner of my eye, I saw a body lying dead still near me. Something terrible had happened; it was my mum.....

SUPER CAITLIN SAVES THE DAY!
BY CAITLIN LYTH

Once there lived a young girl named Caitlin. Caitlin was only nine years old, but she was not little. She had a best friend, Emily; they were the best of friends and together they called themselves Team Cemily. Caitlin and Emily loved nothing more than to sing along together to Taylor Swift songs, their favourite songs being *Style* and *Welcome to New York*.

One day they arrived home from school and there was a surprise waiting for them both. Their Mums had bought them both tickets to see their very favourite artist, Taylor Swift. They were beyond excited.

Two days later the day had arrived; they were both counting down the hours. It was four hours to go and Caitlin's mum broke the news that she had no idea where the tickets were. She began a frantic search for the tickets. She searched the house top to bottom. The girls were starting to become concerned when they heard a loud shriek. Mum had eventually tracked down the tickets with an hour to go. Hoorah!!! They jumped in the car and headed off to Manchester.

Arriving at the arena with just minutes to spare, they found their seats just in time. The atmosphere was building, the crowds frantically waving their posters in the air. Then, with a loud roar which seemed like it shook the building, the lights went up and there she was, standing in the spotlight.

When the first song started there were loud cheers and screams- the tension was building. Throughout the concert the noise was deafening with everyone singing along. The concert went by in a flash and before they knew it, the last song had arrived. Everybody loved it. The song was nearing the end when suddenly there was a very large boom, followed by a strange silence and then loud, piercing screams as crowds were carelessly clambering over the seats with people in a frenzy trying to get out. Caitlin was safely outside but soon realised that her friend Emily was still inside.

Meanwhile, Caitlin -still amongst the chaos- witnessed a young girl being trampled on. She stopped in her tracks and scooped her up and ran with her until she was safely out of the arena. Then Caitlin had a tough decision to make. She was now safely outside himself. Without hesitation, she made her way back inside where, before her eyes, she saw lots and lots of people needing help. She did her best and helped where she could- after all, she was only a nine year old girl. All throughout the night, emergency crew helped to try to reunite loved ones and Caitlin stayed with them to help too.

The following day was like a dream. Caitlin revisited the Arena. Roads were closed and police were everywhere. There were flowers, teddy bears and kind words laid nearby. Sadly, lives had been lost and some families were waking up not knowing if their loved ones were alive. Police Officers provided support for those families that had lost loved ones. One of Caitlin's friend's Mums was looking after one of the families and arranged a very special visit from Taylor Swift .

Caitlin had been a very brave little girl. When she went to school, her friends wanted to ask questions. Caitlin told everyone what had happened. From then on, everyone would talk about the day the very brave nine year old girl helped save lives. From then on, everyone affected tried to rebuild their lives in the best possible way.

You are probably thinking was it a dream; did a nine year old girl named Caitlin really help to save the day!!!

THE MISCHIEVOUS TRIPLETS
BY EMILY HESKETH

Once upon a time in the year 2000, a happy couple were set to have a baby. But they didn't get what they expected; they got triplets. The girls were named Millie, Mollie and Maisie .

18 years later

Millie, Mollie and Maisie had almost finished their schooling. Unfortunately, however, their parents had kicked them out of their house. The girls had no alternative but to go and live with their aunt and uncle who forced the girls to rob and cause mischief.

2 Weeks later

The triplets were forced to go and rob diamonds, emeralds, sapphires and rubies. Their aunt and uncle were very greedy. Refusing to be part of an evil scheme, the girls decided to disobey their aunt and uncle and accept any punishment they received.

6 hours later

Arriving back home from school, the girls were greeted by their aunt and uncle. A long meeting ensued about why they the girls had disobeyed their instructions.

After a lengthy discussion, their aunt and uncle apologised to the girls for having coerced them to participate in their evil scheme. They decided to let the triplets do whatever they wanted to. Mollie chose to work in sports and recreation. Maisie wanted to be an artist. Millie meanwhile, wanted to study geology as she quite liked rocks.

The aunt and uncle learned a valuable lesson and the family lived happily ever after.

HALO 6:
THE UNEXPECTED ATTACK
BY REN SMITH

One fine day, on the *Pillar of Autumn*, Master Ren 118 was at training camp when suddenly, BANG!!! An alien ship hit the Pillar of Autumn. The aliens, seemingly unbothered by the crash, seemed a bit strange though: they were in pyjamas. And the little ones were eating popcorn! "Hu," whispered Master Ren. Yet stranger still, the mysterious visitors had trump guns and stinky gas bombs. "Ew what is that smell?" exclaimed Ren. But it was too late; the marines had fainted because of the smell.

Just then, an alarm sounded loudly in close proximity. ALERT! ALERT! DANGER DETECTED! THERE IS A HORRIBLE SMELL ATTACKING THE INFRASTRUCTURE OF THE SHIP! ALERT! ALERT!

"I must do something to save Commander Smith," Master Ren thought. "Aha, the airlock, that should send them for a flight," Ren screeched. "Open the airlock" he screamed. AIRLOCK OPENING. I REPEAT. AIRLOCK OPENING, came a sound from the computer.

Master Ren clutched onto a rope as the aliens in the bright pyjamas went zooming past him at hyper-speed into the far reaches of space. AIRLOCK CLOSING. I REPEAT. AIRLOCK CLOSING, came a voice from the computer once again.

After that, nothing happened until it was lights out and Ren had gone to sleep. "Ooooh, I'm a ghost. I am here to tell you something," came an eerie voice emanating from somewhere among the darkness. Ren woke, rubbing the sleep from his eyes, pinching himself to make sure he wasn't dreaming.

"Who is that?" he asked.
"It's me! Your best friend, Sam," came the reply through the darkness.
"I knew it was you," whispered Ren, "shush now and please let me go to sleep," he concluded.

The next day was different, however. Normality resumed on the Pillar of Autumn. Nothing bad happened at all. The aliens were a lot quieter. And so it remained.

If there is ever trouble, if ever you have a problem- be sure to look for the one in the grey armour with 118 on the left side of his chestplate. And make sure he has a gold visor. Because, that's me, Master Ren, the Guardian of the Pillar of Autumn.

FOOTBALL
BY FREDDY DOLBY

RETURN OF THE SHADOW MAN:
THE BOY IN THE PHOTOGRAPH
BY MR GRAHAM

I spent five long years in the penitentiary, waiting for my appeal. Sixty months of knowing I was innocent and of not being believed. One thousand eight hundred and twenty six days of being surrounded by career criminals who'd committed the most heinous of crimes. My own mother and father had denounced me and I had been vilified in the press as a monster; a modern day Jekyll and Hyde- normal by day but criminal mastermind by night. Yet none of it was true.

In reality, I was lucky to get my life back. Freed on a technicality, I wanted to forget about it all; to pretend it had never happened, that it was just a bad dream. If only it was that easy. Back in the real world, no one wanted to know an ex-convict. I was left fighting to clear my name, to repair my reputation and to win back my friends and family. With patience and with time, it was a battle I knew I could win- a fight to get back to some semblance of normality. The Shadow

Man had other ideas, however.

In prison I'd led a sedate existence- daily chores, thirty minutes in the exercise yard, a book in the evening if I was lucky. At least I'd not been missing any periods of time. I'd not dared use any of my privileges to access a paint brush or easel. I was haunted by those paintings, those prophecies of doom that had led to my incarceration. Instead, I'd taken up yoga, focusing on finding balance and peace with the world around me and in my troubled mind-trouble inflicted by the Shadow Man. *Who was he? Why had he chosen me?* I knew I hadn't committed those crimes. Certainly not of my own volition.

Leaving prison, I had my clothes returned to me along with thirty seven dollars fifteen cents and a mobile phone complete with cracked screen- a souvenir of my arrest. I flicked the power button on the phone with hope and longing but unexpectant of any sign of life. To my great surprise, it still had charge. It lived to fight another day. A symbol of hope and of redemption for one who needed it the most.

I had just stepped out into the light, a free man, with a sense of optimism once more when I felt it vibrate in my pocket. *Surely not.* I reached for the phone, studying it in the cold light of day. I could barely remember how to operate the wretched thing. I studied the phone, squinting to peer through the cracks on the screen. A text message. An unknown number. An address. *547b West 51st St, NYC.* What could it mean? Should I press delete and walk away?

Or should I see how deep the rabbit hole went? All I knew was that I'd no place to go and no place to be. This was something at least. I had to find out what it meant.

I walked for miles into the nearest town, picking up loose change I found lying on the sidewalk and looking for the nearest Greyhound bus depot. Pleading with passers-by, I scraped together enough money to buy my ticket. I re-examined the address. *Midtown West*. The Theatre district. This was no pauper's palace.

The journey didn't seem that long. You'd think I'd have been keen to soak up the sights, sounds and smells of freedom again. The truth is, I was knackered- exhausted and drained from living a lie behind bars. Disembarking the Greyhound, I weaved my way through the throng on the streets, up Broadway and past the beautiful black pillars of the Gershwin Theatre.

Finally, I reached my destination. This was it. *547b West 51st St, NYC.* I approached the door and was about to knock when I noticed something peeking out from under the door mat. Something white. Small. Subtle. But definitely present. Stooping warily, I reached for the nugget to find that it was a piece of paper, delicately and deliberately folded so as not to protrude too obviously. I opened it delicately as though it were an ancient artifact. *Message me when you arrive.* Momentarily I stood still, confused at the obscurity of the message. It finally dawned on me. The number. The number that had texted me this address. I had to return the text, to let it know I had arrived. The absurdity of the situation dawned upon me. I was on a wild goose chase, propelled by a mixture of hope and desperation. I'd spent my money and had no choice; I was in too deep. I texted the number and waited for a reply.

When nothing had come through after ten minutes, I was all but ready to decamp to find a place to sleep for the night. My last hopes had all but faded when my phone sounded, alerting me to a received message. *Key in plant box.* What plant box? I looked around my feet expecting to see it. It wasn't there. Then, from the corner of my eye, I saw it. A hanging basket. It was the only thing that came close to resembling a plant box. I clawed at it, hoping to keep it still long enough to search inside it. Fumbling in the summer breeze, I was struck by the pretty blue flowers with no discernible scent. Rummaging with more urgency for the key, my eye line drew level with their white inner ring and yellow centre. Completely absorbed in my task, the significance of the petals didn't dawn on me. *Forget Me Nots.* It was a message, albeit subtle. But a message nonetheless. My fingers struck gold. A key, to be exact.

Recomposing myself, I tucked my shirt back into my jeans and put the key in the lock. The door squeaked open and I made my way into the unknown. The hallway was clean and airy. There was little or no dust evident. Someone was living here. At the very least, someone had been here recently. *Hello*, I called longingly. Silence. I continued forward on my quest. One foot after another, the floorboards creaked under me as though they were being woken from their afternoon nap by my sudden intrusion. I turned the corner into the main living area. Scanning the room, I saw that on one side was a sofa, directly opposite a television. A coffee table sat alone in the middle of the room bearing a further handwritten note. *Food in fridge.* I looked at the note closely, searching for any clue that could help identify its author. Nothing.

Driven by curiosity and hunger, I ventured further into the bowels of the house, finding the kitchen. Like the living room, it was clean. Not a lot of furniture or accessories but certainly everything a person could need to survive in modest comfort. The rattle of the fridge freezer waking from its hibernation and jolting into life shook me. I opened it to reveal its treasures. Food. Drinks. All fresh. Someone had stocked up recently. Stocked up for me. The note on the coffee table was clear. *Food in fridge.* I was free to help myself – gifts courtesy of the stranger who'd invited me into their home. A pack of sandwiches caught my eye. Ham and pickle. I scanned the wrapper. The date was good and they looked fresh. I took them from the fridge, along with a bottle of milk, and returned to the sofa in the lounge where I wolfed them down. Flicking on the television, I caught a news bulletin. My release from prison had made the news. It would take time for me to be forgotten. Drained by my adventure and with food in my stomach, I must have nodded off, still unaware of whose hospitality I was enjoying.

When I came to, it was dark outside. Seemingly, I had

slept for hours. Disorientated, I stood up and felt for a light switch. The bulb illuminated the room, revealing my surroundings more clearly. The sofa. The television. The coffee table. It all looked familiar from earlier. Except there now stood in the corner of the room an easel, complete with canvas, paints and another note. *Thought you might like this.* I felt the fear rise from the pit of my stomach, through my chest and the hairs on my neck to my ears and head. All the memories came flooding back in an instant. My previous life. My arrest. The easel hadn't been here when I'd fallen asleep, had it? I was sure it hadn't. Except I couldn't be sure. I doubted myself even though I'd no reason to. I focused on my breathing, calming myself and channeling a sense of peace that gradually restored itself as I sat down and crossed my legs like I'd practiced so many times in my cell. I'd almost fully relaxed myself when it occurred to me that someone had been in the property while I'd slept. They'd left an easel and paints. *But why?*

I'd resolved myself to investigating the rest of the property when I saw a picture frame on a shelf above the mantelpiece. It hadn't been there before. I was sure of it. Standing up again, I approached it cautiously. It was a photograph. Of me. Much younger. With my arm around another child whose face was hidden- coloured over with what looked like black marker pen. I tried to place the photograph. A time, a location, anything. Nothing. Staring at the photograph, I knew it meant something- that there was some hidden meaning. I thought deeply about it, closing my eyes to retrace any sliver of a memory of the photograph. But when I opened my eyes once more, I quickly realised that it was morning and I was in bed. An unfamiliar bed, in an unfamiliar room. Throwing back the quilt, panic set in as I looked down and realised my hands were covered in dried paint. *The easel. The paints. The canvas. The note. The photograph on the mantelpiece.* It all came rushing back, the memories of the previous night seeping into my consciousness like a flood.

Instinct carried me out the door and down the stairs. I hadn't a clue of the layout of this property yet I knew where to go. Bursting into the living area, I saw it immediately. The canvas. No longer blank. A new painting. It was happening again.

With trepidation I stepped forward, anxious about what secrets the canvas would reveal. Would I be back in prison before nightfall? What villainous acts had I depicted with horse hair? As much to my great relief as to my surprise, there was seemingly no crime laid out before me. Instead, I'd painted myself looking at a photograph- the very same photograph that had been in the frame on the mantelpiece last night. Stepping back from the painting, a memory stirred from deep within the hippocampus of my brain. I was able to place the photograph. Elementary School. The day I'd auditioned for a part in a school performance. I studied the painting again looking for any clue as to my mystery companion in the photograph. And suddenly I saw it. There *he* was. In the background of the painting. In the shadow of the doorframe, beyond the open door. *The Shadow Man.* I'd painted a scene from the previous evening. He'd been here- in the room while I was painting- and was behind all of it. I was a pawn on his chessboard, being moved and manipulated into place once more. He was laughing at me, revelling in my misery. I had to stop it once and for all.

I was lost deep in thought when it occurred to me that I needed to check in with my probation officer; it had been thirty six hours. As strange as it might sound, hearing another human voice was soothing. I confirmed my residence at the address in New York and explained how I'd come to be here. Not the truth- I didn't want to be back inside again- but the sort of explanation he'd accept. A good excuse. A plausible one. Hanging up the phone, I resolved to fight the Shadow Man by *not* fighting him. He'd expect me to wrestle him in my mind but I'd not. I'd paint. But I'd control my painting, control the circumstances under which I'd paint. In my heart of hearts I believed that my painting would set me free from his tyranny.

Filled with resolve, I went for a walk to clear my thoughts and to get some fresh air, returning home as darkness set in once more. I'd found fifty dollars in my jacket pocket. It hadn't been there yesterday. *He'd left it there. For me.* I knew it was from him. But I'd already resolved not to fight it so I'd picked up a few essentials and a couple of bottles of beer. I was going to paint tonight. I was going to wrestle back control and use *my* gift to *my* advantage. I was going to bring the Shadow Man to heel.

After dinner, I sat down on the sofa, flicking through countless channels on cable television. My mind was restless and couldn't settle on one programme. I was thinking about what I would paint tonight and how I could seize back control when I realised I was actually standing in front of the canvas with a brush in hand. The framed photograph was now on the coffee table and it had been moved beside me. I looked at my watch. One thirty in the morning. I glanced back at the canvas to see what my hands subconsciously had been busy at work with. It was the assembly hall at my old primary school. Two children were on stage. I recognised myself instantly from the clothes I was wearing- the same clothes as those in the photograph on the coffee table. And beside me was my friend; my unidentified friend. In that instant I decided to return to my primary school in Brooklyn, feeling it held some of the answers I needed. But how would I get in?

Riding the subway in the early hours, I told myself it was a bad idea and in my heart of hearts I knew it was. Wait until Monday. Pay a visit to the school office. As if I could! My release from prison had made national news just a day or two before! Yet here I was plotting to break into my old school building. I convinced myself that it was okay to do a bad thing for a good reason. That anyone could understand. *Tell it to the judge*, I heard my troubled inner voice say.

In the shadow of moonlight, the school building looked exactly as I remembered it. I'd not stepped foot in or even near the place for thirty years. But nothing had changed and it felt as if I had been transported back in time. Mr Archer. Mrs Gemmill. The Farrelly Twins. It was as if the shadow they'd cast remained lingering over the building, haunting it and awaiting my return. Checking the coast was clear, I clambered clumsily over the fence and landed with a thud on the yard. I searched around the old stone wall at the far end of the playground, looking for a loose rock to break glass with. The assembly hall, I reasoned, would still be in the same place- the old Master's Building. There were no visible CCTV recording devices. I looked for a small pane of glass and shattered it with a sharp stone as gently as I could. Brushing the remaining glass away with the stone, I climbed into the building listening for a security alarm. Nothing.

Stepping down onto a hard ceramic surface below me, I quickly discovered that I was in a bathroom. I was certain the staff room was beyond the door and to the right. Opening it, I saw that I was correct and made my way down the narrow corridor to where I believed the assembly hall to be. Rounding the corner, I saw it. It suddenly made sense. The hall was there. In darkness. But a light shone from underneath the door of a small stock cupboard at the far end of the hall. As if a genie had clicked his fingers, I had complete clarity. The school auditions. The art stock cupboard in the hall. The Shadow Man. It all made sense. My unidentified friend was Roderick Burns.

Opening the doors, I relived it all as I entered the hall. I'd been cast as the main part in our school performance- The Spider. But having seen the costume and script, having felt the burning of the eyes of my classmates boring into the back of my head, I'd chosen, instead, to remain an understudy.

An understudy to Roderick. I'd told him he'd be great- that the part was made for him. That he'd be remembered for it. I'd convinced him, out of a sense of self preservation, to stick with it when I found him crying in the art stock cupboard in the assembly hall. I told him that I'd be there to support him, waiting in the shadows. He'd swallowed every word I'd said. He called me his *Shadow Man*, his saviour waiting in the wings- in the shadows. He knew I had a better memory than him. And when he forgot his lines in rehearsal, I'd been there at the side, out of sight, guiding him through his next words. But not on the night of the big performance. I wasn't there. I didn't show up. Roderick had forgot almost all of his lines. He'd wet his trousers on stage. I had been right about one thing: he'd never be forgotten.

My hand had almost made contact with the stock cupboard door and was ready to wrench it open when the light went out. The cupboard was now as dark as the hall. I opened the door regardless. In the darkness immediately in front of me, an even darker shadow hovered ominously at the back of cupboard. *Roderick?* I questioned anxiously. I waited for a response. After a few seconds, confirmation followed. *Why, Roderick? You've ruined my life. Five years, I spent in prison. Five years. My family; gone. My life; gone. Why? Because I didn't show up for a stupid performance to help you with your lines?* His voice seemed familiar but I struggled to place it. But as I listened to his response, I identified it. My probation officer! I felt his words send my head spinning in circles. Was he hypnotising me? I felt my head become lighter and lighter. Twitching momentarily, I realised that I was once more back at the New York address. Looking down, I saw paint on my forearm and fingers and a paint brush in my hand. The photograph was on the coffee table below me. Roderick's face was still blanked out with felt tip pen. The easel! I stepped back and viewed what I'd been up to. There it was. A painting revealing his fate. The school assembly hall filled with police. A man in handcuffs being lead from the hall. A photographer taking snapshots of evidence. Bags of loot. Bars of gold bullion. Some of the same gold bullion that had been stolen from the Manhattan Bank and found in my apartment. It was over. Maybe now, I could finally start to rebuild my life.

ABOUT THE AUTHORS

This is our third volume of stories from children at James
Brindley Community Primary School.
Each and every one of these delightful stories have been
written by children, alongside yet another sneaky one from
a teacher.

Children were invited to submit stories for publication
because we value creative writing and want to encourage
our children to write for pleasure.
We are very proud of everyone that took time to write a
story for our book.

25061056R00076

Printed in Great Britain
by Amazon